ADULTING

ADULTING

NEHARIKA GUPTA

HarperCollins *Publishers* India

First published in India by
HarperCollins *Publishers* in 2019
A-75, Sector 57, Noida, Uttar Pradesh 201301, India
www.harpercollins.co.in

2 4 6 8 10 9 7 5 3

P-ISBN: 978-93-5357-149-8
E-ISBN: 978-93-5357-150-4

Typeset in 11/14.7 Warnock Pro at
Manipal Digital Systems, Manipal

Printed and bound at
Thomson Press (India) Ltd

For my parents

1

Talk to Me About Literature
– TEJAS –

Saturday, 23 May

Today is the beginning of the rest of my life. Three years of traipsing around the continent and I've written a book even I would love to read. It's not everyday that a Delhi University dropout ends up writing a book that publishers bid for. A good book, not a vapid love story. These characters are based on real people, people I've met and loved and known, and more than that, it's a story that's universal: one of heartache.

It was skewed but I smiled.

I smiled at everyone around, whoever was here for my book. We were at a place called Social, in Hauz Khas Village, for my book launch. The entire joint was full of people I didn't know. We were all here, celebrating.

'Tejas! Can you hear me? I need your help,' Ruhi said, beckoning me towards the loo, beside a slumped-over girl in an evening dress. Half of Ruhi's long brown hair was tied up, the other half swinging loose. She looked like her usual elfish self, even in the body-hugging skirt which, it seemed, her mother had picked out for her. More of a ponytail-and-jeans type of girl, she had paired her outfit with shiny sneakers. Ruhi's cheeks were flushed and she pushed her glasses up; they had a tendency to keep slipping down her tiny nose.

'This is Aisha,' Ruhi said, pointing down.

'Nice to meet you, Aisha,' I said to her as she lolled her head forward.

'Please don't joke right now, okay?' Ruhi said. 'We need to help her. She isn't waking up. How drunk are you?'

'Not at all. I'm enjoying this too much sober.' It was true, I was watching people who didn't read for nuts make fools of themselves, trying to talk to me about literature.

'Let's get her to a hospital,' Ruhi said. 'She said she wasn't going to drink tonight. Something else is up, okay? Please.'

'Everyone says that, including me. Who is she?'

'Aisha Oberoi, the new social media manager at Litracy. We've been working together a week now. She officially starts on Monday.'

'Ruhi, you hardly know her. She's not your concern, man. Leave it alone.'

'Tejas. You'd do the same for me, wouldn't you? Please! She's a friend. It's going to be a while before your speech anyway. I'll allow you to cut it short. How about you just read from the book and don't talk about it?'

'Oh hell,' I said. 'You drive a good bargain. Fine, Ruhi. Grab her bag.' I wasn't used to addressing crowds, anything to make that easier was okay with me. I lifted the girl and put her on my shoulder. She was even lighter than she looked.

'Lead the way.'

Ruhi led me to the exit avoiding the prying eyes of the party guests, or Farah, I figured. Ani approached us seeing us heading out. Ruhi told her the situation and Ani said she would help delay things a bit. Ani – or Anandita Sharma – was the head of PR. She was good at her job and got things done but one wouldn't want to get on her bad side. I hoped she wouldn't spill to Farah.

'It was a good launch, Ruhi. The first half hour, at least,' I said, when we were buckled up in the car. Aisha was stretched out in the back of my Audi. 'You should go back. This is your event.'

'Our event,' Ruhi said. 'Ani will help explain things to Farah. I can't spend another minute defending myself for my tiniest of decisions.'

'You still call her that?'

'She thinks it's modern.'

'Sounds like her. Funny how we both are the nexus of this event but want to get away from it.'

'It's best we take a little breather. It'll be a long night,' Ruhi said.

'I'll make something up for Farah,' I said. 'To take the heat off you.'

Farah was the editor-in-chief at White Dog Books, Delhi's biggest publishing house. She was also Ruhi's mother. Litracy, as in Lit-racy, was White Dog's imprint featuring up-and-coming contemporary writing, like my novel, *Carnival of Dreams*.

Litracy was Ruhi's baby. She had the sole responsibility of signing on authors, overseeing the editing, art and production. She ran it like a startup, there were coffee machines, bean bags and fridges stocked with Red Bull and beer. Indeed it was full of some of the brightest, most creative people in town. She had free rein and did brilliantly for herself, but her mother kept a close eye on her. Too close. Ruhi had been groomed for being Farah's successor since school. This was a test.

Farah made Ruhi's life hell, or rather Ruhi let her, in exchange for Litracy, a barter of power between mother and daughter, the traditional and the new. A father figure was not in the picture, having passed away when Ruhi was three. Ruhi would have to put her foot down at some point, lest Farah's rule became draconian, which it was dangerously close to.

'Social media huh?' I asked, glancing at Aisha's face in the rearview mirror.

'She was a real find. I came across her here in Hauz Khas, putting a blog post together. She is one of Delhi's most iconic influencers. Her lifestyle blog is going viral online.'

'Ah, that's why she looks familiar. I read about her. *Very Delhi Girl* or something.'

'*Every Delhi Girl*.'

'Doesn't she have anyone to take care of her?'

'I couldn't spot the people she came with,' Ruhi said, pushing her glasses up again, checking her phone for the tenth time.

'So what's the deal with her? She single?'

'Tejas! She's unconscious.'

'I'm sure she's okay. I mean, she's famous-ish, like me, so just asking, you know ... who she moves with.'

'Bloggers, designers, fashion entrepreneurs, people like that.'

'Good for you, it will lessen the burden of the world for you a bit. Good for me?'

'She knows how to sell a story', Ruhi said. 'I've done my homework.'

'I have no doubt. Here we are,' I said, pulling up at the emergency wing of the hospital. Attendants came out and helped us take Aisha in.

'I'm going to call Farah. You go on ahead. And bring back some gauze,' I said, looking at my phone. 'I need to call Farah, I have four missed calls from her already'.

'Small accident,' I explained on the phone. 'I cut myself on some glass. No I wasn't drinking. Back in fifteen minutes. Yes, Ruhi's with me. She drove me here.'

Ruhi came out. 'Here,' she said, handing me the gauze.

'What's the situation inside?' I asked.

'Don't ask. She's waking up now. She hadn't eaten all day. She has an awful bump on her head and they want to check for a concussion. I was going to introduce her to Farah tonight, but that will have to wait.'

'Ruhi! We're here because some bimbo has been starving herself all day? Now I get why Farah insists on babying you all the time.'

'Shut up, Tejas. Leave my mother out of this. You'd have done the same thing in my place. And you don't know Aisha, okay? We really connect,' Ruhi said, turning away, sniffling. 'Is it so terrible of me to think of someone other than you for five minutes? This entire night was for you. I worked so hard, everything worked out perfectly. It's going to be a great launch.'

'It is.'

I held her. No one was around. I kissed her – a taboo in Delhi, at least when on the road.

I was extremely fond of Ruhi. She adored me to the point of insanity, and was a marvellous editor. I couldn't have asked for more during the six months I spent on nerve-wracking rewrites. Pity we had to keep it from her mother and the entire office.

〜

Sunday, 24 May

After a month of sitting at my computer with nothing to write, I had a damn good confidence boost after my launch last night. It was the pickup I'd been looking for. I began working on a romance as soon as I got home. Love really seems to get the crowds going these days. I'm not sure what to add though, maybe a historical setting or a murder? This cootchie-coo drama is not really my thing.

Eight hours of scribbling and playing with storylines and I was wide awake. I wasn't groggy at all and I decided to visit the hospital to give Aisha her bag. I found it in the car when I was returning home from Social last night and Ruhi had asked me to drop it by her and Farah's place in Noida or the hospital.

The hospital was closer and I wanted to save my day for writing.

I was in Aisha's room now. I looked at her black dress, carefully folded on the side, next to a shaving mirror. Minute snores escaped her mouth, now devoid of the pink lipstick from the night before.

Rubbing her eyes, she took a while to remember where she was, and she was startled to see me.

'Hey, hey it's me. I – I'm the writer with Litracy. I was just leaving.'

'You ... Tejas. Ruhi's boyfriend,' she mumbled, reaching for the shaving mirror by her bed.

'You know.'

'It's my job to know'. She smiled, wincing as she prodded the nasty bruise on her forehead.

'That looks painful.'

'Why are you here? Are you one of those writers who overshares and posts too much personal info on social media?'

'Hell no, I don't use social media if I can help it.'

She shook open the bun on top of her head. Black, gold and light-brown locks cascaded down to her elbows. She tousled her hair over the bruise. Even in the green hospital gown she was stunning. No wonder all of Delhi had fallen in love with her.

'This' – I pointed at her purse, a little explosion of pink, no bigger than my palm – 'We left it in the car when we came to drop you.'

'Oh. Why did you wrap it in newspaper?'

'Uh, I had to walk by a lot of people to get to your room,' I said, to Aisha's amusement. 'I'm glad I'm making you feel better.'

'I missed the entire launch. How was it then, up to your standards?' Aisha asked.

'If it were up to me, I wouldn't be addressing an audience at all. But decent, I guess.'

'What are you writing?' she said, pointing at my Moleskine. 'You carry that around?'

'Yes. Musings.'

'What now?'

'Observations and thoughts. Notes. I take them all the time.'

'Thoughts. Even we have those,' Aisha said. 'Though the rest of us don't get paid to think, unfortunately.'

'But you do. Aren't you my social ehmm–'

'Social Media Manager.' She raised an eyebrow at me. 'And it's *not* just about Instagramming and Tweeting all day.'

'I didn't say anything,' I said.

'Oh sure. You thought it.'

'I guess you get that a lot.'

'It's what, eight in the morning? Do you always wake up this early?'

'Yes.'

'And write all day?'

'At times.'

'Can you–' She struggled to reach her bag on the table next to her.

'Here.'

Aisha took out her phone from the bag and began flicking through a photostream, on Instagram, while simultaneously plying me with every question she could think of.

'Do you have friends?'

'Of course.'

'I didn't see any last night.'

'It's not their scene.'

'Where are your parents?'

'London.'

This got her attention. 'Nice. Mine travel a lot too. So do your parents have property in London or what–'

'Yes. They switch between there and Delhi. I'll be going now. Mail me your questions okay? I don't like interviews and reporters. It's very early in the morning and I'm a little hungover.'

'Hey, no. I'm not trying to spring anything on you. Just getting to know you. I like Ruhi and I'm curious about you. It's like black and white coming together, you and her. Plus, we're going to be friends too, obviously. We'll be working together a lot from now on.'

I must have rolled my eyes because she said, 'I'm not bad company. I've been told people love me.'

'Sweet nothings.'

'Excuse me?'

'It's what sycophants do. You know, people who flatter.'

'I know what sycophant means. Are you implying what I think you're implying? I have plenty of friends who don't care about the fame.'

'Sure. So do I.'

'Stop with the sarcasm. I'm good with people.'

'That I believe.'

'Let's change the subject. How's your next book coming along?'

'Okay. I'm halfway through.' That wasn't exactly true, though that was what I'd been feeding Ruhi and Farah.

'What's it about?'

'You'll have to read it to know.'

'Forever a mystery', Aisha said. 'We've spent minutes talking. And I don't know a single thing about you.'

'Yes.'

'Yes? Who talks like that?'

'I do.'

'I give up. I'll just ask Ruhi.'

'Is that the message *Every Delhi Girl* wants to give to the masses? Aisha Oberoi: a quitter?'

'Not by a far stretch of your strange imagination,' she said.

'Read my book, the first one. That's all you'll ever need to know,' I said, leaving Aisha to her phone.

At home, it was back to the drawing board for me. I'd promised Litracy a second novel. I'd been up since five trying to chart out a decent plot, and was going nuts.

Whatever I came up with was overdone and the words just weren't coming out right.

It was going to be another torturous day of trying to figure out the plot, and I'd have to drink myself to oblivion yet again and go through my ideas, hoping a story would stumble out of a drunken haze and fit into the already-crumbling love story. Whatever happened to those carefree writing days when I wrote *Carnival of Dreams* with ease.

I was going to be out of time soon. That wouldn't be good for me or Ruhi. She put all her faith in me, signing me on. A wave of gloom came over me and I poured myself a whiskey.

2

Ideal Delhi Girl

– AISHA –

Sunday, 24 May

What's on your mind?

Stoked about my new job with @LitracyBooks. Thanks @RuhiSingh for the fab opportunity. Let's go viral! #WhiteDogBooks #LitracyBooks #HKV

I have been fake-smiling so much at the hospital staff, it hurts. Attendants kept barging into my room all night, waking me up, asking if I was okay. Then they would harp on about if there was someone I could call. No, my parents were too busy and no, I couldn't stand anybody I did know. Not in this state.

As it is, my ex Kartik and his sister Kareena had disappeared during the party. Probably gone to a bar in

HKV and gotten drunk. We had free drinks at the launch, what was the big deal in showing me a modicum of support ... where was the love I'd shown their million-and-one ventures? Ruhi got me to the hospital. Tejas drove me, and came by this morning to return my bag. He doesn't talk much – I had to pry things out of him – the complete opposite of Ruhi.

The first time I met Ruhi Singh, I thought she was in school, or at the most, first year of college. She was wearing white sneakers with a white t-shirt and jeans. I thought she was an intern at one of those startup types, looking to feature a product on my blog.

Turned out she wanted to hire me. Hard to believe this tiny girl was the force behind Litracy Books. She took me around the Litracy office, an entire floor of a building that had a coffee shop at the ground level and an up-and-coming e-zine on the first floor. We were up on the second floor with fab views of the village and the lake.

She explained how publishing houses were starting to have their own personalities and that White Dog Books was a huge MNC, but Litracy, an imprint, was unique to Delhi, with room for experimentation and play. She wanted to make Litracy its own entity, and she wanted me to do for Litracy what I'd done for myself.

I was right for the job, no doubt. In the five months since I'd been home, I began blogging and people loved it all: how I looked, what I did, where I went, my makeup, skincare routine, everything. I didn't even know there was a following for this sort of stuff. And then, I started contacting cosmetic companies and PRs of nightclubs and there was no looking back. Since the beginning of April though, I felt like there was something missing. Maybe it was to do with being without my parents, without my college lifestyle, back in Delhi after almost five years. I needed stability. So I said yes.

I tweeted about my new job – which actually starts tomorrow – and it was overflowing with congratulatory messages. There are 263 likes already. It made me think of the numbers had I actually been at the launch last night, but Ruhi assured me there would be more opportunities to show off my social media skills.

It was 11 a.m. A doctor should be coming in now and discharging me soon. That's what the on-call doctor told me last night.

Sure enough, a lady walked in.

She looked to be in her mid-thirties. Tall and thin, the lady looked at me with a piercing gaze. She was wearing a fitted floral shirt with black jeans. There was a white coat over her arm and she had a coffee flask in the other.

'Hi, I'm Maya. How are you feeling today, Aisha?' she said, going to the window and pulling open the curtains. Sunlight streamed in, lighting up the room.

'Ready to be discharged. I don't have a concussion. Only a nasty bruise that makeup isn't going to hide for a week.' I pointed at my forehead.

She smiled and poured her coffee. Black. Strong.

'That's a good kind of problem to have, considering.'

'Do you recognise me, doc? I'm Aisha, from the blog *Every Delhi Girl*.'

'Ah, that's you. Much more vibrant in person. And I'm not a doctor.'

'No?'

'I'm a nutritionist. I deal with people who eat, or don't eat, their emotions. And I meant presence you know, not looks. You have more of an effect in person. Like, vibe-wise, you know?'

'Oh. Wow. That's nice to hear. So can I ...? There was way too much milk in what they gave me and it did not smell like any kind of coffee at all...'

'Oh yes, of course!' Maya rinsed a cup and poured me some coffee, then settled down on the couch with the clipboard at the end of my bed.

'Where are your parents?'

'Abroad, travelling for work. I stay on my own. Always have taken care of myself.'

'I'm sure.'

'Why are you here?'

She tapped the clipboard. 'Your blood work.'

'I wasn't drinking. You won't find anything fishy in there.'

'I didn't find anything, actually. No sodium, no potassium, hardly any iron. Forget about magnesium, calcium and phosphorus. Did you know zinc is an essential mineral for the body too?'

'Oh. Hmm. So I need to drink more water.'

'Are appearances very important to you?'

'I like taking care of myself.'

'That has to extend to your body, Aisha. Not just how you look in the mirror. You are slowing down everything in your body. Hypothetically, in an extreme scenario, if this were to continue, your body would shut down completely.'

'Whoa. This is not an extreme scenario.'

'It could be.'

'I love my body, I love how I look.'

'Maybe too much.'

I felt like I was under a microscope, I realized Maya was one of those people you couldn't spend too much time with. Too much pressure to say the right things, one wrong move and you disappoint them – and they would tell you so.

Maya spent a good thirty minutes giving me a lecture. She was an LSR graduate, super into ideologies and stuff. That coupled with biology and nutrition, my head was spinning with all the information. My body was stressed, she told me, and this was a wake-up call. I had to set my own standard and focus on fitness before thinking about adhering to any standard society set for me. She pointed out how even a single day with not enough food in my system had left me unconscious. I had to continue visiting her and change my diet completely.

It was hard to believe at first, but not that hard, looking back at the year I'd had. Having returned to India in January, I'd had just over a month of regular eating with my parents. Come March and they were off again to spend three months in some remote village in northern Italy, making wine and writing another book together.

My diet was a mess after they left, what with me promoting my blog and partying 24/7. Now that I'd just started working, I had had no time to recover or 'listen to my body', as Maya put it. Sure, that explained why my stomach was rejecting tequila and vodka, and I'd been stuck with wine all of March and April. But I'm only twenty-three. I'm supposed to bounce back in no time. I will.

I will switch my diet around and start exercising if need be. But there is no way I will be putting on fifteen kilos like Maya insisted. I have always been the Venus in every room. I can't be chubby and graceful at the same time. Have you ever seen a fat ballerina? It doesn't work that way.

Not to mention, the source of my name and fame, my blog, was a beacon of beauty, something that Delhi girls held precious. It had to reflect an ideal Delhi girl for readers to aspire to be. Holding up a mirror to *every* Delhi girl was not my intention.

3

Love Gaps

– RUHI –

Monday, 1 June

To Do:

Litracy
- *Fix epson covers colour for current 2 comics with In-house designer*
- *Conference with Ani about T's book sales and marketing*
- *Suggest LGBT author for DU talk*
- *Schedule meeting w designer #2 for next 2 adventure comics – delegate*
- *Send final pdf of historical fiction to author – delegate*
- *Proof detective novel #3 – delegate*

Mountain Echoes
- *Finalise Tejas's panel with Siyahi & brainstorm topic*

- *Decide which authors, books to go and how many copies, if any, to be signed*
- *Revise list and see if any other authors are available to go*
- *AIS for all 12 authors and novels – delegate*

'Ruhi? Are you here with us?' Farah said. 'Would your mind like to join us today?'

'No. Yes,' I mumbled, covering my list with my elbow. 'I'll get in touch with Siyahi.'

That got me a look.

It was two weeks after Tejas's book launch and we were sitting in our monthly edit meeting, something I detested. On the first Monday of every month, my mother would come in to the Litracy office instead of the White Dog headquarters in Gurgaon. I hated these visits as Farah would come in, throw her weight around as editor-in-chief, and undo weeks of work.

I had a vision for Litracy, and a plan in the back of my notebook while still an editorial assistant at White Dog Books. I believed that the future of publishing was in creating a niche, indie, author-driven market, like the comic book and graphic novel publishers abroad. There were far too many people writing all kinds of things. People had enough choice and would begin to bore of the half-witted romances and must-read literary novels and would gravitate towards genre-bending writing by authors who really had *it* – that X factor. It was already happening with music, people had their own signature taste. Even Apple Music and Google Play were using listener preferences to suggest songs to users.

A whole year of ideation and reader statistics went into creating a world-class presentation complete with an AV. Farah was impressed and let me present it to the Asia Head and I was assigned for a trial, which, a year later, has been going superbly. I thought my dog days were over, but Farah's micromanagement has only intensified.

We were discussing representation at Mountain Echoes, the litfest in Bhutan, as the book was creating a lot of buzz.

I'd told Farah before the meeting how much Tejas hated public speaking and to not push for a big audience to start with.

He was scowling at the room, looking everywhere but at Farah. Aisha was looking resplendent in a sheer aqua tunic that reached her ankles. My mother had chosen to wear blue with jeans too, and was pleased at this symmetry. She was in awe of Aisha and had warmed up to her over the past fortnight.

Aisha gave her good reason to. She was the only one appearing attentive out of the three of us, jotting down notes with her long, manicured fingers.

She and Tejas were on either side of me while Farah sat across from the three of us. We were at the only conference table in the office and had a view of the lake.

The rest of the gang, which included two designers, sometimes Ani, and a few interns, were in the office on the floor below.

I know my opinions about my mother were very strong, but in spite of my doing a great job, she never got what Litracy was about, or if she did, chose to regard it with disdain. She played with her hair, nodding at a point

Aisha was making. It was a hairstyle out of *Cosmo*, which she'd taken along with her to the salon. Like a blunt chin-length cut that highlighted the severity of her face. I'd suggested a softer look, but she'd turned it down. Hard on the inside, prickly on the outside, and now her hair was edgy too.

She spent the remainder of the meeting ignoring my points, focusing on Aisha and Tejas, though frequently checking to see if I was paying attention.

Two years working with her and I still wasn't used to her berating. It was one thing at home, but in the presence of my colleagues: entirely another. It always put a dampener on my day. Luckily I had better things to occupy my mind with, like being in love.

Back in February, I was intimidated by the brooding author we'd signed on. I'd met him only once and he'd hardly email back or talk for very long on the phone. This went on for weeks and weeks until I decided to meet him and talk about the edits we wanted from him. He wouldn't come to the office so I had to go see him at his house.

Tejas's place was lavish. He lived alone in a farmhouse-mansion in south Delhi. His parents were hardly around so the house was mostly full of his stuff.

There were rooms with papers and notebooks of writing and rooms with books. His dining room was full of drafts and the sitting room with poems.

His book, *Carnival of Dreams*, was a series of vignettes, of characters and places he'd come across. We'd considered making it a memoir but taking into account his next book, which was to be fiction, we decided to launch him as a novelist. This gave him more creative freedom for his book as well.

When we began editing, he'd prefer meeting me at his home. My mother assumed I was 'building a personal relationship' with the author, like all editors ought to, and a *very* personal relationship developed.

At the beginning, I was startled by his strict schedule of waking at 5 a.m. and writing till 11 p.m. I guess he had a lot to say.

Even when I reached early on a Sunday morning, he'd have breakfast ready and be sitting with a book.

As I got to know him, I found him increasingly interesting. He'd read everything from the Harry Potter books to Greek mythology. He said I was the first person he showed his poetry to.

When he told me he liked me, I did not know how to deal with it and didn't meet him for a week. I have to admit, Tejas was not the kind of guy I expected would go for a girl like me. I could only ascribe one word to him: intense.

I had only known him some twenty-one days when I began exploring the possibility in my head. I needed time.

He was very cordial and took every opportunity to make me feel comfortable. He even emptied out a room for us to sit in and I'd notice there'd be a different book collection each time, which he thought I'd like to read and let me borrow from.

Months after working together, I found a handwritten note he'd put among my things asking me out. It was during the week we sent the book to press and I gave in.

He'd cook for me often, and on days when I was stressed, he'd spend hours patiently listening to me whine about my mother. Not that he'd talk much anyway, but he'd make me feel welcome in every conceivable way – something I found myself needing outside of home, more and more.

'Let's grab lunch, guys?' Aisha said, snapping me out of my daydream. Farah had finally left. She had a working lunch in the city with a publicist.

'Sure,' Tejas said. He never had lunch in the office. Things were changing for me – how much a few kisses could do.

I had the usual: a bowl of salad from home and a cold coffee. Tejas got black coffee and a sandwich from the cafe below.

Aisha opened her three-tier tiffin box and spread out a salad, a bowl of curd and steamed vegetables. She began clicking pictures of the spread.

'I was prescribed this by a nutritionist,' she said, by way of explanation. 'She wants to keep track of my diet.'

'I hear you were in New York,' Tejas said. 'What's it like to be back?'

'Good, but I miss everything about it. I had to find things to do here. I put all my energy into my site when my parents left.'

'Left? Left you alone?' I said.

'I've been on my own since I can remember. Boarding school, college hostel, summer schools. They love to travel.'

'Aren't they worried about your safety, here in Delhi at least?' I said.

'It's a safe community. And I'm really good at taking care of myself. That night was a freak incident,' Aisha said, looking at me. 'I can take care of myself. My parents are okay with it. Different people, different parenting.'

'I didn't mean anything by that—'

'It's okay, Ruhi. It's tough for some parents to see their kids grow up,' Aisha said. 'It's no secret around here that Farah makes office tough for you.'

'I don't care about that. I just don't like hiding our relationship. I don't like hiding anything.'

'Ruhi. You're not used to being independent. When you do, you'll stop guilt tripping,' she said. 'You're as codependent as your mother is.'

'Hmm...' I finished my lunch quietly, pondering over this.

Codependent? *I. Was. Not.* She didn't know a thing about me or my life.

Tejas found me later and could tell I was upset. He took me to the cafe and we talked over macaroons till I felt better.

~

To Do:

Once there was a boy whose face was tanned with the sun of seas beyond. When he smiled he was remembering a different time and place. The clothes on his body never really seemed to fit, they were mere conformity. His journal was his most prized possession, a companion to life, and it made me jealous. Did this man have an identity of his own? Or was he made up of his travels, nothing and everything at the same time...

I'd had some three cups of coffee after lunch and finished everything on my list. I had three dedicated interns helping me and was done for the day.

Our operations at Litracy were small, there was only editorial, design and now social media, which were in-house. Marketing and finance of all imprints of White Dog were handled by the big teams at the WD headquarters in Gurgaon. Even the production of our books was done at the WD printing presses.

This gap between work, which never happened at WD, was precious and not infrequent at Litracy. It was when the best brainstorming took place. However, this day, this gap was being filled by thoughts of a dashing author I knew.

I tried to concentrate as Aisha talked. She was working on an article and told me I was perfect for 'Makeover Madness'.

'It's a monthly feature on my blog where I give one lucky girl a makeover, so she can channel her beauty from outside to in. I've done it for all my friends. My followers love it.'

'Ah. Um. Well.'

We were in our glass-walled office. Aisha was pacing the room, talking and planning. I shuffled together the papers on my desk and started correcting a manuscript proof.

'Haven't you noticed how differently people treat you when you're dressed up?'

'Sure.'

'It's even better when how you're dressed comes from deep within, like self-expression. Like Tejas and his book.'

'Uh-huh.'

'Ruhi. I can tell, your mind is elsewhere.'

'Oops. Sorry, Aisha.'

'If I didn't know better, I'd say you were thinking of a certain writer. Come, let's get some fresh air.'

By fresh air, Aisha meant a smoke. We headed out to the staircase where she lit a cigarette. I didn't smoke, but I could use a break. It was going to rain and the weather was perfectly romantic.

What a wondrous feeling, to be lovelorn. I could stay with it forever. I told Aisha about the day I first met Tejas.

It was a chilly but sunny day in February. The office was quite empty. He was scheduled to meet me and was early, standing outside and smoking. I wanted to stand in the sun but somehow felt shy and pretended not to recognise him. I tried to rush inside when he stopped me and introduced himself.

I felt my cheeks grow warm and I couldn't help giving Aisha a goofy smile as I told her this.

'Go on,' Aisha said.

'It's so good to talk to you about this,' I said. It was.

Since I'd been dating Tejas, I'd had to protect my love like a little Gollum. I couldn't talk to my mother about it, nor Ani, and did not feel like confiding in the designers either. Within office hours, I'd keep my feelings pushed to the back of my mind, like the box of keepsakes from our dates that I kept in the back of my cupboard.

I had filled the box with things like a copy of *Carnival of Dreams* that was personally addressed to me, the hand written note T had written, a box that once held a muffin he got me, and lots and lots of dried flowers from his place.

It was filling up and like my mind, I didn't have space to properly place things there anymore.

There was no one I could talk to about this who wouldn't blab, till Aisha came along. With her, I felt lighter and happier.

'What if you guys end up going to Thimphu together?' Aisha said, making a heart with her fingers. 'Finally some alone time.'

'With Farah? It would be like nightmare on each street. She'd make me plan everything, then get mad at me for not doing it her way.'

'Whoa, Ruhi! Biased much?'

'You've seen how she treats me.'

'Yeah,' Aisha said. 'And Sonam and George and Vicki. Your interns.'

'I'm not new. I've been working here for a year and at White Dog for another year before that. And more importantly, I'm her daughter. No respect.'

'She may not want to play favourites in your office. Respect for you.'

'She can play nice.'

'What do you do at home together?'

'Eat. Watch TV. Sometimes.'

'Oh no. What about movies or meals out?'

'We used to, before I joined Litracy. Not anymore. I like spending time working on Litracy. And now, Tejas and I catch up every night.'

'I'm sorry. What will make you feel better?'

'Tell me about this blog thingy, it sounds fun.'

'So, three or four different outfits, two locations. We can shoot it here and maybe one more place. Are you writing that down in your list?'

'No, Aisha, don't!'

'Is that – poetry?'

'No, just...' I sighed. 'I can't stop thinking about him, Aisha.'

'Earth to Ruhi. We have a problem.'

4

Gritty and Indie

– TEJAS –

Tuesday, 27 June

I wonder if I can pull off horror. It's not really my thing, but who knows? Anything to keep my mind off of the coming event. Maybe a horror novel about public speaking. Hmm. Though I will have to address crowds in Bhutan, a change of place would be nice. Good thing it's Mountain Echoes, not the crowded JLF.

I was on time. I blew on my coffee, waiting for Farah and the girls in the conference room, a floor above the girls' office.

Situated in a cul-de-sac of Hauz Khas Village, it took me all of thirty minutes to get to the Litracy office from the other side of Delhi in the morning. It was raining. Ruhi had called me from the office at 8.30 a.m., an hour before office began, and told me to get there by 10 a.m. Her voice betrayed good news.

It had been six weeks since I'd been to the Litracy office. I didn't like the place but always took an opportunity to meet Ruhi.

She'd spent the last two weeks hinting about Mountain Echoes. Litracy was working on organising a book reading there.

Ruhi was the first to enter the room. She looked pleased with herself.

'Mr Sahni. Good morning.' Farah entered. 'The newspapers and magazines reviewers have been swallowing your book like a happy pill. Your reviews are stellar and the book is appearing in listings and recommendations. We want to confirm you for the litfest in Bhutan. The tickets are in ten days time, the first week of August. Is it okay for you to travel for a few nights?'

I nodded.

'Very well. Aisha is available that weekend for live social media updates, and since you are the only Litracy author going to Mountain Echoes, Ruhi will be accompanying the two of you.'

I hadn't expected on seeing Farah today. Ruhi hated these surprise visits or 'snoopings', as she called them. I knew, I had to hear her vent about it frequently. But this was good for Ruhi, a chance to get on the festival circuit on her own.

Farah wrapped up the meeting soon after and wanted to see the social media scheduling. She went to Aisha's desk with her on the floor below us. I was pleased she didn't ask me how my next book was coming along. But Ruhi did.

'Are you thinking about going with the romance plot?' Ruhi said when we were alone.

'I'm going to comply with inspiration and see where it takes me.'

Over nights of endless chatting on the phone, I'd told Ruhi about my inspirational woes, having sugar-coated them of course.

'Good. Well, decide in a couple of weeks and start writing as your next book is due at the end of the year,' Ruhi said, as she put in her Bluetooth device and started clicking away at her phone. On the conference room intercom she instructed the Litracy interns on the rest of the day's tasks and then turned her attention back to me.

'I can't believe she's letting the three of us go without her,' Ruhi said. 'It doesn't seem like my mother.' She glanced at the empty space at the table where Farah had been sitting.

'Things change,' I said.

She leaned back into the crook of my arm. It was only us on the floor, we could see if anyone came up the lift or the emergency staircase through the glass walls of the boardroom.

'You know, if this goes well, I'll be able to get on the core team for the Jaipur Literature Festival in January.'

'Ruhi, that's huge.'

'Yes. In ten years, I want to be Festival Director of my own litfest.'

'Considering your drive, you could get there sooner.'

'There's no Farah sitting on your head, is there?' Ruhi said.

'She's not all that bad now, maybe this will help you. You could try being at ease around her, one day at a time.'

'I'm good now that she's not here.'

Ruhi had been tense all through the meeting in Farah's presence. Now she was like a kitten lounging around.

'What do you talk about at home with Farah?'

'Oh office gossip, author tantrums, the news. It's only at work she gets unbearably bossy and annoying.'

We heard the noise of the lift coming up and Ruhi jerked herself away from me. It was only Aisha.

'I had some things to go over with you, Tejas. He's free now, right?' Aisha asked Ruhi. 'Or I can come back later,' she winked.

'It's okay. I, uh, I was just leaving,' Ruhi said. 'I have to speak to Farah before she leaves.'

All through the meeting, I couldn't stop looking at Aisha. I knew she'd been trying to put on weight. Over the past weeks Ruhi couldn't stop talking about how well Aisha was handling the diet, with her blog and office. The way she went on, it was as if she was infatuated with Aisha. True, Aisha had put on a little. Not that I was one to judge, but it suited her.

Today her hair was carelessly tied up, bangs were falling over her face and the back of her neck. Her face had more definition.

Aisha whipped out her notebook.

'I've been talking to Ani – it's tough to get any info out of her, so fill me in if I miss something.'

'Yeah, she has a personality.' I omitted the word 'attitude'. Ani was the PR and marketing manager at White Dog, Gurgaon, who divided time between WD and Litracy and had helped Ruhi organize my launch.

'Is that a web-chart?' I said, looking at clouds with words like Twitter, Blog, Insta inside them. 'Reminds me of school.'

'It's a mind map,' Aisha teased. 'Get with the times.' She was sitting on my right.

'You don't have to do a thing. Just talk to me time to time. I know you aren't into sharing details about your personal life. I'll help you filter what to put out there. You can just tell me about a typical day in your life.'

'Well, I don't have any typical days.'

'Hm, how about what you eat, where you like to chill with your friends, your weekends.'

'I'm not gonna do th—'

'Hey, I get it. You need your creative space. But think of all the readers who idolise you, who've spent money on your work. It's to keep you in their memories. If you want to stick to your writing influences, that's cool too. Traditional works. I promise everything I post will be gritty and indie, like your book.'

'I can work with that.'

Then Aisha spent way too long looking at what I was wearing. Top to bottom.

'Real subtle.'

'Yeah, I'm just trying to get a sense of your style.'

'I don't have a style. I'm a guy. I have a wardrobe.'

'Little do you know. There are guys out there, straight guys, obsessed with themselves and what they wear, to the point of annoying even me.'

'It's hard to believe. And how exactly do you intend to use Pinterest with my writing?' I pointed at her chart, my hand bumping into hers, which jerked like she'd been electrocuted.

'Sorry I, uh, sort of bumped it. You know, when I fell,' Aisha said. That 'fall' was more than a month ago.

'I want to reach your readers through all the platforms they might be using,' she added.

'Hm. Here's something for you: spin it however you want,' I said.

She leaned in, and I caught a whiff of leftover cigarette smoke. Hers or mine, I wasn't sure.

'I can read people.'

'What now?' She was taking notes.

'I'm not an extrovert but I'm good with people. I spend hours observing people, it transforms my writing. I can plug my ears, look at two people talking and explain the dynamic between them. It's useful when I'm around someone who likes me.'

Aisha inched away from me instantly. 'Uh. Um. Okay, in Thimphu, I'll follow you around a bit, see what you do,' she said, consulting her notes. 'We can post pictures, interact with your fans.'

'I value my privacy.'

'I value your sales.'

'Touché. Here's what. You still haven't read *Carnival*. Read my book and we have a deal.'

'Done. Oh and I never thanked you for that night, taking me to the hospital.'

'Ruhi made me. But yes, anything to get out of a party.'

'The friends I came with turned out to be complete ditchers.'

'Ruhi is a good friend to have.'

'I'm happy for her. She really likes you. Maybe crossing over to the dark side is good for her.'

'It's not that dark, she's still rainbow Ruhi,' I said. 'You should have seen her before we met. She was like a walking-talking publishing house. On cocaine. She wouldn't go anywhere without her computer and Bluetooth device.'

'Do you ... do you think her work would ever affect her life? I only ask you because, I mean, her mother...' Aisha paused. 'We need lives outside of work too. Farah is great, but she's married to her job. And Ruhi may be going the same route, I think.'

'Yeah?'

'I'm not trying to gossip, just—'

'I think Ruhi's problem is not callousness, it's the opposite. It's being too concerned with other people's feelings. She's the most passionate and also one of the most stressed people I know. She likes her status as the youngest managing editor in town a lot. But yes, chilling out would do her a world of good. Like you. I know it seems like the world is eating out of your hand and it must take *some* work. But there's no drama.'

A blush was making itself evident on her cheeks.

'Thanks. Okay so this is what I've worked out,' she said, pointing at her chart, brushing off what I'd said. Was I making *her* uncomfortable? I imagined she'd be used to attention and it would be the other way round.

'This is how I've linked all your social media together, through an app called Hootsuite.' She explained what the best kind of posts were and what grabbed the most attention and at what time.

'Though you don't have to worry about that,' she continued. 'All you need to do is write. And spend a couple of hours each week interacting with your fans and approving what I email you.'

'Whatever you need.'

'This was super easy,' Aisha said, snapping her notebook shut. 'Not at all the cryptic author everyone says you are.'

'I am,' I grinned. 'You just have to get to know me.'

5

Better Ugly Than Dead

– AISHA –

Saturday, 6 July

What's on your mind?

How awesome is it to be working with the most eligible bachelor in publishing? Find out in my Q&A with author @TejasSahni @TheLiterateWhiteDog – Litracy Books's official blog. #LitracyBooks #WhiteDogBooks #TejasSahni #Travel #Fiction

My hands were shaking uncontrollably and for the past ten minutes, I had been struggling with my mascara in Maya's office loo.

Makeup was my best friend these days. My clothes had stopped looking good on me a while ago. As of today, even my fans had forsaken me. I could not be home alone. I didn't know how to deal with all these feelings, I had not had this kind of problem before. All I could do was touch up my face every half an hour to avoid having a panic attack. I couldn't get my mind off all the nasty comments I'd seen on Instagram today.

My friend Kareena, the model, wasn't answering her phone. Neither was Kartik. Ruhi was tied up with work till afternoon, so I decided to meet Maya. At this point, talking to anybody would do.

I hadn't met her for a while and she'd been on my case to visit her this week.

At the beginning, she'd been super nice, but crazy strict, worse than any teacher I'd ever had. She wanted to meet me every week, know every ingredient I'd ingested, and would keep calling and calling till I actually got to the appointment. She'd stalk me on Facebook and Instagram, to see what I was up to, liking everything, till I began to fear I'd see her wherever I went.

She asked me to send her photos of every meal I ate, refusing to believe I was following her diet.

The only thing that made her happy was the increasing numbers on her weighing scale. So I went to her appointments wearing my baggiest jeans with chunky jewellery beads stuffed into the pockets, my iPod and iPhone in the back pockets, and clothes layered with tank tops and tights. I'd sweat till I reached her office, but God, she had a powerful AC. She thought I was in a weird emo-fashion phase. This got me through for a while.

Of course, I was eating fruits, drinking water, my weight was increasing a few hundred grams every week, but I did not *want* to put on real weight. Why would I?

I had planned to continue with the charade until one fateful day, when I was driving home from work – contemplating buying little weights to put in my shoes – when I lost control of the car and blacked out in the lane leading out of Hauz Khas. Then I heard the knock on my window. I had been blocking traffic for ten minutes. I told the policeman my head was spinning, and took nearly half an hour to recuperate. He assumed it was that time of the month for me. 'Lady police officer *ko bulaoon*?' he had said. The car had a nasty scratch, which was a small price to pay – literally. But I couldn't handle the feeling of losing control.

That was when I realized that the only way out was trusting Maya and changing my weight. I tried not to think about when things would get ugly. I'd probably have to work out like crazy every day. *Oh well, better ugly than dead.*

I was Aisha Oberoi. I had created my brand out of nothing. I was one of *Vogue India's* 'most sought-after Delhi bachelorettes'. I could deal with the situation. Taking a deep breath and smiling at my perfectly-made face in Maya's loo, I headed back into her waiting room.

Maya was finishing up with a client, a skinny, pimply teenage boy, who couldn't take his eyes off me. In recognition or admiration? I couldn't tell anymore.

She signalled for me to come in. Two green potted plants framed her desk and behind it was a poster of fruits and vegetables in the shape of a heart. I felt queasy just looking at it.

'Aisha, you didn't have an appointment today. All okay?' Maya said.

'I didn't want to be alone,' I said after a moment. 'I'm sure you saw.'

'I have been noticing some of the things people are saying.'

There were scores of people commenting on my latest blog post. It was called 'Working Beautifully' and was a montage of my best office outfits shot at various places within the Litracy office. True, I was visibly chubbier than I'd ever been before, but I did not look unseemly from any angle in those pictures. It was only now, in July, that I truly felt like I was a little on the fatter side of the population.

It had gone live this morning and I'd had to spend every waking minute moderating the malicious comments like: *Big, fat and juicy. Don't work so hard, just work out. Fat-ass Aisha. You're not confident or interesting anymore, I'm out.*

'I feel sick,' I told Maya.

'Did you eat today?' Maya said, taking off her glasses, looking younger instantly.

'I mean, I feel disgusting. *Fat.* I can't deal with this anymore, I can't. People are posting shit, I don't fit into my clothes, I have cellulite. I don't know what to do. I don't look like myself.'

'It's hard, I know. Weight is an emotional issue for most people,' Maya said. 'Not physical.'

'I am *not* most people. I just wish my stupid followers didn't have to care so much about how I look. And judge me for it. I'm not forcing them to look at me.'

'Have you thought about writing about anything other than yourself?'

'No. That's me, it's what my blog is about.'

'Body-shaming.'

'Huh?'

'Body-shaming. That's the term for what people are doing. You're under direct attack as your blog is about lifestyle.'

She pushed a bowl towards me. 'Almonds?'

I took one.

'People do that to singers, dancers, news anchors, makeup artists, anyone who puts themselves out there. If you're an RJ or a poet or a doctor and you're on social media, it's going to happen to you. I want to say you are catering to people who are obsessed with looks and you shouldn't expect any better, but it's just not true. You could be an editor-in-chief like your boss Farah, put a video of her online, people *will* be commenting on her appearance. In fact, it's not just body shaming. People are intolerant of each other in general. It's something you're going to have to get used to on social media.'

'That's a very pessimistic view of things. I don't accept it.'

'Have people always talked to you about how great you look or how perfect your hair is all the time? Has anyone ever written you off as one of those too-much-makeup or airhead type of girls?'

'If they have, I haven't noticed or I don't care. That's their reductionist view.'

'Isn't your motto *self-expression through fashion for every Delhi girl*? Pretty big thing, self-expression. Did anyone ever discuss that with you or has any interviewer ever asked you about fashion as an art form or even what direction your blog was going to take in the next few years?'

'Umm...'

'Sorry to break it to you, dear. Ageism. You'll face sexism. Prejudice if you're married young, if you're not married young. If you're a mother, if you're not a mother.'

'That sounds like a difficult life.'

'You learn to deal with it. You've been dealing with it ever since you were a child, Aisha. You're just tasting it now. And life goes on. How do you feel this week?'

'Stronger. But I look like crap. When I felt like crap, I looked amazing.'

Maya laughed. 'Take the good with the bad. That's the only way this is gonna work. Now, for the moment of truth.' She pointed to her weighing scale. I got on. It touched fifty-six.

'Aw man, this sucks. I don't want the bad, only the good,' I said. 'How much more do I have to put on before I can start losing it?'

'You know what, come back from your work trip and you can start gymming. I'll give you a new diet and you can tone up what you don't like. Working out won't necessarily help you drop the kilos, but it will make you fit and will take commitment.'

'I don't care. As long as I look amazing.'

'This is for you.'

'A notebook?'

'A diary. I give it to my clients to write down what they eat.'

'I'll just send you a picture.'

'Actually, it may help you to write down how you feel. You're trying too hard to define yourself instead of letting it happen. You're smarter than that. Remember, people will always find flaws. No one really cares that much, no matter how much hate they spout on social media, Aisha, and that's a good thing. They do go back to their own lives eventually and so should you.'

'Social media *is* my life.'

'My point exactly. You are more than just a social media mastermind.'

~

Sunday, 7 July

What's on your mind?

Out with my girl and publishing visionary @Ruhi Singh people-spotting and coffee-drinking at @DLFPromenade Delhi. Come say hi!

'Hazelnut cappuccino?' The barista asked. I was at one of my favourite coffee shops, Mocha Arthouse, at the DLF Promenade Mall in south Delhi.

'With skimmed milk. And that cookie, please.'

I was waiting for Ruhi. We had a shopping date to buy formals for the Mountain Echoes litfest and finish my blog's makeover segment. I'd driven straight here after meeting Maya. Ruhi wasn't having the best day either and sounded like she was having one of her anxiety attacks, and this one was related to Farah mentioning she should dress like an adult for the litfest in Bhutan. Farah had a wicked sense of humour, but most of the time Ruhi was too emotionally raw from pleasing her to catch on. I'd been to Mocha before with boyfriends. Malls, for me, were the happiest places in the world, and I could do with some cheering up too.

I've always wanted to take those vertical coffee shots and I told the barista handling the froth to make a swirly 'A' on top. I had a while to kill so I walked around looking at Steve Madden and Zara with my coffee.

I mulled over my meeting with Maya. We were living in a world of specialisations. Hers was nutrition. Mine was social media. That was my universe. How was I more than that? Did she not understand how it all worked? How had she made it, by fluke?

As if the universe was responding, I noticed a group of schoolgirls, looking over at me and pointing. I swear, the skinniest and tallest of the lot had hair exactly like mine, right down to the balayage highlights.

'Hi.' I flashed them my signature smile. They followed the tall girl to my table.

'OMG. You're totally my idol,' she said, obviously the leader. Did I sound like that?

'Can we get a selfie?'

'Of course.' I took out my phone, and each of them insisted on using her own as well.

'Will you follow our blog?' the second one quipped. She was wearing four-inch heels. Even I wouldn't dream of wearing those to a mall.

'Sure, what's it called?'

'*Every South Delhi Girl.* The three of us run it together,' the third said. She was carrying an oversized LV bag like mine, but she looked like she could fit inside hers.

'Shut up! That is so cool.' They nodded. I spotted Ruhi waiting, looking at the four of us, hesitant to approach.

'Look, it was awesome meeting you guys, but I have to go now.' I gestured at Ruhi.

'Who's that, your colleague?' the third girl said.

'That's Ruhi, my friend. She's the managing editor at Litracy, you know, Farah Singh's daughter.'

That didn't make an impact on the girls, though I know it did on Ruhi. She was silent all the way to Smokehouse, the restaurant we were lunching at.

'Unoriginal of them, *Every South Delhi Girl.* But still. Gotta love the enthusiasm. Don't you think so Ruhi?'

She didn't say anything.

'You know, I've started to blog about eating out and publicising places. Food blogging is big, you know.'

'Hmm...' Ruhi silently listened to my prattling all the way up on the escalator till we reached the restaurant.

'Table for two,' I told the waiter. He led us to a table by the window. Ruhi looked minuscule sitting in her chair, her shoulders falling forward. It was as if the incident had shrunk her.

'Ruhi.'

'Yes,' she said, fiddling with her watch. 'Tejas is not a bachelor. Why'd you have to promote him like that? You know—'

'I know, Ruhi, but your mom pushed for that idea. It is a good way to pitch him, it would be odd not to use it. So many of his fans are women. It's about sales, nothing else. Just tell Farah. You're an adult. If this affects you, it's only 'coz you know you're worth more. And it's not like Farah doesn't know what a hard worker you are. You're the one who doesn't own it.'

The waiter brought us the menus.

'I will have the smoked chicken salad and the grilled salmon followed by the cheesecake. Bring the first and second courses together please. I'm a little hungry.'

'I'll go for the caesar salad,' Ruhi said.

'Any main course or dessert for you, ma'am?' The waiter asked her.

'No, thank you,' Ruhi said.

'Try something fun, why don't you. A pasta? What do you recommend?'

'We recommend the wild mushroom fettuccine if you're vegetarian, and the chicken risotto in non-vegetarian.'

'The vegetarian, please,' Ruhi said.

'Any drinks, ma'am?'

'I'll have the smoked cosmo.'

'Same for me,' Ruhi said and we handed our menus back to the waiter.

'I can't think right now – a little rattled,' Ruhi said.

'I can see that.'

'It's also to do with responsibility. I don't get any. You know what I need? I need to be on the JLF core team. Then she'll take me seriously.'

'I'm all for you moving up the corporate ladder. But JLF is six months away. Why is that important to you? You have a lot to do on a daily basis and you do a phenomenal job and none of this has anything to do with you being honest with your mother.'

'I'll get a lot of responsibility and the ability to show everyone what I'm capable of. If I get on it, I'll be handling all the authors and possibly be on a panel. Everybody would know me. Farah would not be involved much. I'll directly report to the Festival Director—'

'Ruhi, we all act like Farah's a she-devil, no offence. I know I do,' I said. 'It helps to bond in the office. Don't tell me you don't know this. At the end of the day she has to answer for a lot of things, everything you and I do actually. She's not out to get anyone, and it's not like you assert yourself anyway, Ruhi.'

'That's why I want to let my work do the talking.'

'Too much work makes Ruhi a dull girl.'

'Let's talk about something else,' she said.

When the food arrived, I asked the waiter to click a picture of us with our meal. I use the tag #Delhicious for myself, and now more appropriately, for food posts. Ruhi gave me half her pasta.

'By the way, you could report that comment,' Ruhi said.

'What comment? There are so many these days.'

'That guy who said: "Does this mean you're more fun to ride now"? That's sexual harrassment.'

'I'm not reporting anything. It's the big bad world of the internet,' Aisha said. 'I'm letting it go. I don't care what hotmale-underscore-sixty-nine thinks of me.'

'I admire your tact.'

'You know everyone has confidence issues, including me.'

'I find that hard to believe,' Ruhi said.

'It's true.'

I didn't mention I'd been avoiding shopping alone for weeks.

'You have to try this,' I said between mouthfuls of the cheesecake. 'Mouthgasm.'

Ruhi dug into the dessert with a vengeance, the first sign of enthusiasm I'd seen all day. Enough play.

'So ... I was speaking with Tejas the other day. He thinks you need to chill out.'

'What can I say? Got a publishing house to run.'

'I think you need boundaries. You can't be as invested as you are in a job or a relationship, Ruhi, your life revolves around things. A dozen authors, that's it. And an acquisition a month. I'm handling all online media. You need some time for yourself. Like, live a little. It's gonna help your relationship with your mom too.'

'I can't, okay. It's not me.'

She was beginning to clamp up. I would have to try a different approach. I let her finish my cheesecake and we walked out of the restaurant, back into the mall and entered Forever 21.

Ruhi was to be the star of a makeover segment I was planning for *Every Delhi Girl*. I'd made myself responsible for unearthing her personal style, something she could carry forward, while wowing my subscribers.

She disappeared into the clothes racks, moving camouflaged behind the ankle-length dresses.

Ruhi was like a tiny, wild animal in a jungle. Having selected five pieces of clothing, she stuck to them, come what may, and walked straight to the dressing room. She was not like most people, myself included, who would grab one thing here, another there and try on clothes, like personalities, in the changing rooms, dressing and undressing, having personality makeovers at will. Shopping with her was, I hate to say it, like work – something to tick off her to-do list.

I left her and adopted a zen-like approach for a while, and began browsing. A simple peacock-blue dress would do for me, and I picked a size six. Once a size zero, I did not look forward to undressing my skinny 'personality' in the dressing room and confronting a big girl. The lingerie, however, I was keen to try, and I headed towards that section.

There I spotted Ruhi, looking at a black lacy low-cut blouse, something she'd never be able to buy with Farah. She was just staring. Not holding it, or looking for her size or feeling the material. Just staring.

I had a feeling Ruhi had to be nudged into this next phase of her relationship.

'Hey,' I said. 'Try it, let's have some fun.'

6

In My Feelings

– RUHI –

Sunday, 7 July

To Do – 1st Half

Shopping:
- *Work outfits*
- *Lingerie*

To Do – 2nd Half:
Work
- *Check email*
- *Finish slush pile of manuscripts*
- *Trend research & catch up on other publisher's news*

'That's more your style,' I said, before regretting it immediately, looking at an extremely sexy black blouse that

I could never pull off. Aisha's waistline had expanded in the last two months. I didn't want to bring attention to it. Not today. After all, she was spending the day with me. I'd never had such days growing up. My mother would pick out everything for me, in her words: leaving me to do more important things with my time.

Aisha swivelled towards me, a purple sheer blouse in her hand. 'With your frame and skin tone, you could totally bewitch every day with zero effort. If only you had the temperament.'

'I do. I love my pinks and yellows. My style is very Betty Cooper.'

'Then why are you wearing so much black?'

'I don't know. No time. Late night work.'

'Late night work or texting?'

I ignored that. 'Tejas likes me no matter what I wear.'

'I don't wanna give you another lecture today, but you have to start dressing better and for *yourself*. You can do better than wear the same three faded black things to work every week. Isn't that why Farah sent you out shopping in the first place?'

'Mark Zuckerbeg. Steve Jobs. A lot of smart people wear the same things every day.'

'Okay then buy five new black t-shirts and wear them everyday. I swear I've seen holes in your clothes and not the fashionable kind.'

Aisha was right, I could dress a little more professionally. The changing room was small, with mirrors on three sides and a curtain for privacy.

In my sports bra, nothing would entice any man. It made me feel like a teenage girl. The thought of Tejas seeing me like that freaked me out. I knew that wouldn't be happening anytime soon, but I couldn't imagine it happening anytime at all.

'Oh God, what are you, twelve?' Aisha said, bursting into the dressing room I was using, holding at least a dozen hangers.

'Hey, you can wait outside.'

'I can see even more of you now,' Aisha said grinning into the mirror.

'Out!'

'Okay okay, dear prudence, I'll wait outside. Just let me try this on,' she pulled off her blouse and began buttoning up the purple blouse.

'Whoa.' I was looking at Aisha's chest.

'Yeah, I know, perks of putting on weight.' Aisha said twisting and seeing the shirt on herself in the mirrors. 'You can get the same effect with a push-up bra. Wanna try? You'll be surprised,' she said, sliding back into her clothes.

'Just wait outside,' I said, picking a hot-pink dress.

'I'm going to be ready with my phone.'

Sixty minutes. I felt like I was being given a Hollywood-style makeover. Aisha was taking photographs of me to post in the 'after' section of her blog. We'd already shot 'before' at work.

'When is it going to be online?'

'Tomorrow.'

'Yikes.'

'It's gonna be great! Now start stripping.'

Aisha kept bringing me more clothes till I told her I was going to run out of money and patience.

When we finished, I was wearing a bright fuchsia blouse and a cream blazer and had three more bags of shopping. It wasn't hard to appreciate the neat cuts and clothes without virtually any creases. I definitely looked like an editor, or at least a professional.

'What now?'

'Lingerie time.'

I was quiet till we reached the innerwear section.

I was only now beginning to realise the enormity of the situation. I was an adult yet I felt like a kid trapped in a woman's body. Not that my womanly parts were anything to compare to Aisha's. I had 'feelings', of course, when I was with Tejas. It was confusing though, I had no clear answer what to do. And I did not like being surrounded by the skimpy thongs and multitudes of bras in addition to the turmoil in my head.

'How are your friends?' I asked Aisha to distract her from the topic. 'The ones who came to the launch.'

'Don't ask.'

'What?'

'They're really just people from the fashion community. Kareena models part-time and they own a label together. It's called Mystique. They're all right, we were never close though.'

'Kartik and Kareena right? I thought they were cool.'

'Is there anything or anyone you don't like?' Aisha said, fishing in her giant bag for something.

'No I mean—'

'Hmm. Apple?'

'No. How's your diet going?'

'All right.'

'When did you meet your nutritionist?'

'Today, before coming here.'

Aisha fished out a square silver sachet from her bag.

'Here. Hang on to this,' she said, giving it to me.

'Aisha!'

'You know what it is, don't you?'

'Shhh! What is wrong with you?'

'You should be prepared. Looking good in the sack is one thing. Safety, entirely another,' Aisha said, shaking it impatiently like a sachet of sugar.

'Take it. It's for you.'

'Stop it, people are staring.'

'They're staring at you, not me. Haven't you ever put it on somebody? Okay, don't tell me you've never seen one before?' Aisha said.

'Put it away.'

'Okay,' Aisha said, turning away. I went back to looking at the lingerie. I took deep breaths to calm myself.

A minute later she came up to me, tapped me on the shoulder and put the sachet in my hand.

'Yuck!' I shrugged it off like an insect. It flew up in the air and into the pile of clothes the trial-room attendants were hanging. They began giggling immediately.

'Oh God, Aisha. What did you do?'

'Look, they want to keep it,' Aisha said, giving them a thumbs-up.

'Are you trying to be mean? What is wrong with you?'

'Ruhi, I ... misunderstood. Aren't you serious about dating Tejas?'

'Yes. I don't know. I don't think he would pressure me. I'm not ready.'

'Ruhi, you still have to tell him.'

'I don't understand what's going on. I've never been in a serious relationship before, Aisha. I didn't think about the intimacy part. I would die if Tejas left me. I'm going to do everything right. I just don't know what I want, Aisha. Is that a crime?'

'I think you do. If you're ready, you're ready; if not, you're not. It has nothing to do with him. Ruhi, it's more important you have this conversation with yourself, more than me *or* Tejas, so you don't get carried away or do something you'll regret. And I'm here no matter what happens. But you gotta be honest with yourself.'

I nodded.

'I'm heading to the changing room. Get whatever, dealer's choice.' She smiled.

I grabbed a pearly-white bra-and-panty set. I'd have to start somewhere.

Aisha's head poked out from the changing room.

'Ruhi, you gotta help me. I can't zip up this damn dress,' she called out.

'Are you sure it's the right size?' I said, entering the stall.

'Of course it is. Don't be ridiculous. It's a six, even though I'm a four.'

'Well, the zipper is not going up,' Ruhi said.

'It must be stuck. Try harder.'

'I can't, it's—'

'Oh you're useless! I'll do it myself,' Aisha said, grabbing the bottom of the dress with one hand, the zipper in the other.

'No!'

'Oh!' The dress split and the zipper ended up in her hand.

'Damn this stupid dress. Damn this stupid diet,' Aisha said, peeling off the dress.

'Aisha—'

'Leave.'

I waited for her outside, preparing what to say to her. No attendants were around. When she emerged, it was like the incident never happened.

'Ha! That was funny, wasn't it?' she said. 'Babe. I just realised, I have to go. I'm super late for my appointment with Maya. Don't worry about me, I'm fine. I'll see you on Monday.'

'Your appointment was this morning.'

She didn't let me finish, just gave me a quick hug then marched straight to the manager. She gave him a mouthful. I figured she just had to yell at someone. She flung the dress on the counter and walked away. Only Aisha could convince the manager the dress was the store's fault.

Monday, 8 July

To Do:

Litracy
- *Send 2 adventure comics to press*
- *Send historical fiction pdf to press*
- *Track T's sales and amp up*
- *Proof next 2 adventure comics*
- *Send final proof of Indian detective novel #3 to author*
- *Induct new batch of interns*

Mountain Echoes
- *Finalise Tejas's panel with Siyahi & brainstorm topic*
- *Decide which authors, books to go, how many copies, if any to be signed*
- *Revise list and see if any other authors are available to go*
- *AIS for all 12 authors and novels – delegate*
- *Bookmarks*

The 'Makeover Mania' post had a hundred views already. People knew Aisha and followed her blog. Maybe that would help with Litracy's visibility. Anyway, I knew I would feel good all spruced up in my new clothes anyway.

I scrutinised my wardrobe. A black blouse, a fuchsia blouse and three white shirts hung next to my dozens of t-shirts.

It was going to be the black shirt with jeans today. Baby steps. I grabbed a pair of black stiletto heels, three inches high. I'd seen Aisha in six-inch ones the day of the launch.

I'd reach work in time but my mother had her monthly meeting at Litracy, and she'd left thirty minutes ago. We were to finalize all details for Mountain Echoes.

I piled up pages of the book called *Sparks* I'd been editing – a new writer we were picking up – and had brought home for the weekend.

Books have always been my escape. Throughout school they were my most reliable companions, be it the Harry Potter series, *Lord of The Rings*, the Inheritance series, and even *A Game of Thrones*, before it became mainstream.

Far from being a young genius, I hid myself beneath worlds of broomsticks, dragons and magical destinies to avoid undue attention at school. The thick black-rimmed glasses I began wearing at the same time stuck with me through college and after. This helped me perfect a look for a career in the world of publishing that I already had the pedigree of.

When I reached office, my heels shook crazily as I walked up the stairs. I had to take two trips to get my laptop, bag and the manuscript to my desk.

Aisha took one look at me and said, 'Your admirer, he's coming today, isn't he?'

'How do you walk in these damn things?'

'You don't,' she said with a wink. 'Oh, you saw my media plan for this month, right? I've gone through your logistics. Tejas hasn't been emailing or checking his social media. But we can worry about that next week. What else do we have to know for the meeting?'

'Has my mother had her morning coffee yet?'

'You worry too much.' Aisha rolled her eyes at me. She was wearing an oversized shirt, knotted at the bottom, with ripped jeans. Her makeup was light, hair tied back. Her overall appearance was subdued and I was the only person in office who knew why.

When we entered the conference room, Farah was on the phone but she glanced appreciatively at Aisha. If I'd worn torn jeans to work, I would have been told off.

We sat across her, leaving a seat in-between for Tejas.

'No, no. I am not disputing your position as the author, baba,' Farah cooed. 'The epsons were signed by you. I'm looking at them right now. We cannot pull it off the press. I guarantee we'll make these changes in the next print run.'

I wrote 'Minutes of the Meeting' on the top of my notepad in pink ink.

Farah caught Tejas's eye when he entered. He then winked at me and sat at the head of the table instead of between me and Aisha.

'I am not having this conversation if you're going to be like this. Please call me after four. Thanks.' She held up a finger at Tejas, shaking her head as she spoke on her phone. 'Idiot,' she said after hanging up, and took a deep breath.

'You. Take minutes,' my mother barked Aisha into action. 'This meeting's notes go to the CEO.'

I scratched out the 'Minutes of the Meeting' I'd written. I was getting nervous.

Sitting up straight, I crossed my legs and put both arms on the table, exactly like Aisha.

'It looks like all our work is paying off. And thanks to Aisha, we know you'll have a solid turnout in Thimphu,' Farah said. She failed to mention me.

'I can hardly wait,' Tejas said.

'Let's go over a few things.' Farah looked at her checklist. 'The books have reached the shop. You girls are carrying the bookmarks. They turned out well, didn't they, Tejas?'

'Pretty neat,' he said, twirling the samples around.

'Have you spoken to our contact in Thimphu? She was expecting your call this morning,' Farah asked me.

I had no recollection of being told any of this before. I knew sleeping in was going to cost me.

'Didn't you know? You have to coordinate with Pema. Stay on top of things, Ruhi, we've been planning this for a while.'

'Okay, okay. I'm on it.'

Farah went over the itinerary next but I couldn't focus. I looked through my emails but there was nothing in there about Pema. I'd also reached work at 9.30 a.m. sharp every day the past month, except this morning, which in all fairness *was* the beginning of the official work day. How could I have missed such a development? I didn't care what Farah or even Aisha thought, but I couldn't look bad in front of Tejas.

'Aisha, could you please sit with Tejas and preplan all your social media tags and links, hashtags and whatnot. Schedule everything if you have to.'

'Sure.'

'Now about your panel discussion. Pema will be moderating it.'

'I like that I'm going to be talking about travel, and the topic is expansive. The guide says I can cover anything, From *City of Djinns* to Jack Kerouac. I already have notes.' Tejas said, looking positively excited. 'And Mayank Austen Soofi on the same panel. Just. Wow.'

'I've seen his notes. I was going to go over that again with him now,' I said.

'Sure,' Farah said. 'I'd like to see them too. Tejas, send it to us when you can and get started with the social media thing please. We'll work on it and email you back our comments, Tejas, if you want to use them. Aisha, you can take him to the cafe or wherever.'

'This way, Mr Sahni,' Aisha said in jest.

'Please, call me Tejas.'

I wanted to evaporate. Wasn't it enough that Farah was treating me like a kid, she had to treat Tejas that way too, read every word of the speech? Why didn't he say anything back, make a sarcastic comment?

I sat in the room with her, fuming, while Tejas and Aisha skipped away into their social media sunset.

7

Dashing Misfit of a Writer
– TEJAS –

Monday, 8 July

I haven't written anything the past week. It's just too hard. I have been reading a lot though. It's keeping me sane. Lots of inspiration. I must have spent some ten grand at the bookshop. I'm going back to fantasy and crime fiction after years. It's a great feeling. Maybe visiting the girls at the office will help pull me out of this funk.

I lit Aisha's cigarette. We were on the emergency staircase, Litracy's unofficial smoking area. The office, which was pristine white from inside, was butt ugly from outside and behind, like much of HKV's buildings. How much could one do with tiny blocks of balconies and facades anyway.

'How are you doing?' I asked. 'You know, diet-wise.'

'Peachy.' Aisha sat down next to me. Her body was changing, it was getting softer. She was wearing a loose shirt, a boy's shirt. Was that something one bought in a ladies apparel store, or was it an old boyfriend's?

'Looking forward to Bhutan?' She smiled. 'I never thought I'd say this but I can't wait to try their cuisine.'

'Ha! Ruhi won't get to set foot outside the venue. Farah would be tracking her every move.'

'You don't come across as the type to be very schedule-bound either,' Aisha said, giving me a sidelong look.

'Fishing, Aisha?'

'I'm not. But I try,' she said.

'Do tell,' I asked.

'Getting to know you.'

'It's a long story. When I sent Litracy my manuscript, they were quick to sign me on, dispelling all formalities. Within six months, they introduced me as a writer to the publishing world. As thrilled as I was, they also got to expand their repertoire to include me, a dashing misfit of a writer. Their author list has very serious people. This upped their ante. I'm grateful for Litracy taking me on.'

'Why do you sound like you owe them?'

'I should have been smarter while signing the contract. I promised them two books. Not that I don't want to write one more, it's just too soon. On the upside, I got a book and met Ruhi.'

'Well, well, think of the devil,' Aisha said.

Ruhi sauntered in. She was out of breath, her face was an incontrovertible look of melancholy. It was an expression I couldn't have put down, if I tried.

'Looking for Tejas?' Aisha said.

'Hiding from mom.'

'Ciggie, Ruhi?' Aisha broke the silence.

'Sure,' Ruhi said.

'You don't smoke,' I said.

'I'd like to try.'

'Trust me, you don't.'

'Don't tell me what to do, Tejas. You don't own me. She doesn't own me. No one does.'

'Um, I'm gonna be inside,' Aisha said.

'I hate this job.' Ruhi glared at me. 'Lighter.'

'Aren't you a little old for this? You don't have to prove anything to me or your mother.'

'Who says I'm trying to prove anything to anyone,' she said, grabbing the lighter. She tried to light it, without success.

'Suck in while you light it, not too much—'

She began to cough. I thumped her back. She pushed my arm away and stood up. The heel of her shoe slipped between the metal stairs. She struggled to get it out and ended up barefoot with the shoe still stuck. Losing her balance, she fell, half on me, half scraping her leg against the staircase.

'Hey-hey-hey.' I pulled her back up, dusting her jeans and pulling the heel out.

'It's okay.' I pretended not to notice when she wiped a stray tear from her eye.

'Do you still want to try one? I'll light it this time.'

'But I dropped your lighter,' Ruhi said in a high voice.

'No worries. New shoes?'

'I thought of trying something...'

'Uncomfortable?'

'New,' Ruhi said.

'I see.'

'Oh, what did you think of the makeover post? Did you see it? I think my mother liked it.'

'Uh huh.'

'Be honest. What did you think?'

She was looking at me with her giant eyes under those hipster glasses.

What was I supposed to say? It looked like she was trying too hard.

'That style, it works for Aisha. Yours is more subtle.'

'Oh.'

'You told me to be honest.'

'I liked how I looked, for a change,' Ruhi said, pouting.

'You don't have to give me an explanation.'

'I'm not.'

'You don't need to look like everybody else because Farah says so. Or even Aisha.'

'That's not what I'm doing, Tejas.'

'I like the ugly duckling,' I said before I could stop myself. Ruhi abruptly stood up, leaving my hand.

'Asshole.'

'No. I didn't mean that, I wanted to say – I may be completely wrong.'

Shoe in hand, she headed off inside, her little nose in the air. *Girls.*

Monday, 8 July

In a coffee shop
...that I was whole and not broken I would not shatter, I
am not made of glass in the ocean without direction ... There
is nothing in this world that could break me.

My wings appeared and so did everyone else's
I never knew they were there
So
The airplane dreams made sense. I never crashed, I was
just trying to get somewhere better
What I did not realize / Was that falling fast / Was the
fastest way
For change to begin

I was sitting in the cafe below the office. Ruhi and Aisha
were sitting at a different table. I was working on some
poetry, and on a hunt for inspiration. There were enough
people around to observe. A lot of them didn't know me,
or were too busy to be starstruck by my presence. I sat
by myself with my Moleskine poised to pick up bits of
conversation. This helped spark off pages of writing when
I was doing my book and I was hoping it would work now.

I couldn't hear Aisha and Ruhi but I could see them well.
Ruhi was no doubt telling Aisha how terrible I was.

A bit of breathing space was good for both of us.

I went to get a black coffee, and found Aisha sitting at
my table when I got back. Ruhi was gone.

'She's super upset, Tejas.'

'I don't know what to say.'

'You can talk to her.'

'Look, Aisha – it's a family thing. I've been watching her for months. You can't fix it in one go, trust me, I've tried. She is so sensitive, the closer we get, the worse this is.'

'Hey guys.' It was Ani. Tall and thin with a body to die for, she had an opinion on everything. I did fancy her the first week I knew her, but then my interest died out. I never did find out whether she was really into me or not.

'How are you, Tejas? I trust the newbies aren't treating you too badly.'

'Can't complain. How are you?'

'I feel I'm getting old, surrounded by all the old writers we keep signing. You're lucky you have such a young team on your case.'

'Your tea's getting cold,' Aisha told Ani.

'Are you feeling okay, Aisha?'

'Perfect.'

'Come see me later, I have a few tricks you could use – like drinking honey lime water and green tea every morning.'

'Whatever for, Ani?' Aisha was getting impatient, and I was getting to see office politics.

'Oh, you know, to prevent bloating and stuff. It hurts to see all the hate on your website these days. Really.'

'You're no less with your green tea drama—' I began saying.

'Don't speak for me, Tejas,' Aisha said, turning to Ani. 'I don't think I'm going to take advice from someone who still hasn't heard of bras.'

This was a dig at Ani's voluptuous chest – which she loved showing off – and it hit the spot. She left, sulking. Aisha was upset too, though she was doing a fine job of pretending otherwise.

'Whatever,' Aisha said. 'I just came to tell you, I've had a word with Ruhi. She's better now, just be nice at your end. Look, there she is.'

'Excuse me,' she said as Ruhi came towards us.

'Sorry about earlier,' Ruhi said, wanting to talk. 'You have a right to your opinion. Maybe I overreacted. I hope you're not mad.'

I wasn't mad. Just wondering if I had a ticking bomb on my hands.

8

I Woke Up Like This

– AISHA –

Friday, 25 August

Aisha's Journal

The days I feel bad about myself, which have started becoming more and more, I play up my mood spending ten minutes smiling in the mirror every morning. Ruhi is being a gem about the dress and says I'm growing as a person, my personality is getting bigger, and obviously I needed bigger dresses to fill, not those measly little clones of dresses I and every other girl at a party would wear. I liked the thought of that. Tiny dresses, too small to contain me. Then why does growing bigger make me feel so small...

'Hey, I've never seen you writing before,' Tejas said, leaning over Ruhi's empty seat in the aircraft. She had gone to stretch her legs. Tejas looked suitably stubbled and groggy for the 6 a.m. flight we were on.

'It's a journal. I used to write on and off, I've become regular at it now. Do you journal?'

'All the time. I lost mine yesterday though. Don't let that happen,' he said, shaking his head.

'Maybe you left it in the office.'

'I texted Ruhi, it's not there. What are you writing?'

'You know journals are private.'

'Ah, I see. Who you writing about, in that case?' Tejas said.

'You. And how you're turning my sweet friend into a vampire.'

'It's just dark circles, and not just because of me,' Tejas said.

'Maybe a change of approach is required, so, um, Ruhi feels a little more "relaxed" in life?' I said.

'You're paying quite a bit of attention to what I'm not doing.' Tejas said. He shifted from the aisle to the centre seat. 'I am flattered. It was only a matter of time.'

I wasn't sure if Tejas was mocking me or flirting with me. I couldn't help but wonder. Maybe in another life.

'Hey, I know you and Ruhi are tight. I wanted your advice on—'

'This flight is so crowded.' Ruhi was back. 'Everybody wanted to pee together.'

'I changed seats. I hope you don't mind?' Tejas told her. 'I had some questions for Aisha. Here is your orange juice.'

'Sure,' Ruhi said. She was on a roll. Five minutes away from Farah, she had turned into a female version of Tejas.

Cut-off jeans, lots of kajal, a skimpy black spaghetti, she was like a wild child. She was talking to the guys in the aisle next to her, laughing and giggling.

'She's just having fun,' Tejas said, an amused expression on his face. 'Rebel without a cause.'

'That's Delhi's darlingest editor and talented publisher, needing approval from guys, our Ruhi Singh. Who knew?'

'I don't think she had a lot of such attention growing up,' Tejas said. 'Unlike some people.'

'What are your questions? You wanted some advice?' I said before he could elaborate. I don't know why he made me uncomfortable. That was the last thing I needed to be; I'd dated guys more attractive than him.

'I think Ruhi is too serious,' Tejas said.

We glanced at her, her hand in a Bhutanese guy's hand, some game they were playing. Reading palms or something.

'Hmm.'

'I mean serious about me. Too serious. I'm not a commitment-phobe like every guy in a Hindi movie. But I mean, I can't even disagree with her about anything without fearing she'll change her mind, just for my sake.'

'I didn't want to say anything, but I agree. I think this behaviour is actually healthy,' I said, pointing at her. 'Interacting with guys outside her circle. Maybe you could slow down, or take a break – only if you think so, though. I know things are tough with her at home. She is relying on you so much for emotional support, she may get to a point where she can't make a personal decision on her own.'

'Yes, maybe you're right. Let's keep this conversation between ourselves, okay?'

'Of course,' I told him. Tejas soon fell asleep, drooling on Ruhi's shoulder.

Ruhi was having a blast away from her mother, hardly anxious at all, and I didn't want to spoil her fun. Nor did I want her to do anything stupid. I was going to discuss sex with Ruhi. She was so emotionally fragile. The worst thing that could happen was her actually deciding to take my advice of being with Tejas physically on this trip.

Right when I fell asleep, Tejas elbowed me sharply.

'Ow. What?'

'Wake up. Look, its Kangana Ranaut. Ruhi spotted her. She's sitting two rows behind us in the opposite aisle.'

I walked to the loo. There was an air hostess serving a passenger in front of me, so I got a good look at her. How thin she looked. Her waist couldn't be more than twenty inches and her thighs were as thin as my arms. Tejas was standing behind me, also curious to see her.

It wasn't as if I wanted him to look at me, but I was used to the eyes and attention of everyone around to be on me. A knot in my stomach began to tighten. I made my way to the loo and threw up my breakfast. When I went back to my seat, I didn't feel like making conversation with either of them and sat with my eyes shut, pretending to sleep.

Three cups of coffee and two glasses of water later, I was all wired up in the bag collection line. I told Tejas and Ruhi about the plans I had for Litracy and my blog for the weekend.

On returning from the loo, while Ruhi and Tejas waited for the bags, I did my best not to spend too much time thinking how much like a movie star – tall, thin and beautiful – I'd been only two months ago. On my trip back from the loo, a group of local students walked past me. All the girls wore midriff-baring blouses with fitted high-waist jeans. I felt unkempt in my tracks and loose white t-shirt which said *I Woke Up Like This,* something I loved when I bought it.

Back in line, everywhere I looked, I saw young foreign girls and women, looking svelte and completely at ease with themselves and way better than me.

'Ruhi, something's wrong.' I grabbed her shoulder. 'I'm dizzy.'

'What? No, hang on. Tejas. Tejas. Aisha's going to faint.'

Each grabbed a shoulder while I collapsed on my knees.

I woke up to splashes of water.

'You okay?' Tejas said.

'Yes. Now I am.'

'Come, we'll sit down. They'll call us when we're up for immigration,' Ruhi said, linking her arm with mine.

Attendants at the airport helped me to a seat and offered me juice and fruits, fawning over me, till Ruhi thanked them and sent them away.

'Have water to start with. And here, eat this.' She gave me a piece of chocolate.

The warmth of the chocolate enveloped me like a blanket. I didn't say a word in the taxi from the airport to the hotel.

9

A Lady Doesn't Kiss and Tell

– RUHI –

Friday, 25 August

To Do:
- *Create a WhatsApp group for 3 of us & F & Ani*
- *Connect to litfest official wi-fi*
- *Make sure T's notes are in order*
- *Keep business cards*

'This won't do, Aisha,' Tejas said, setting down the big binder Farah had me carrying with us.

'We've spent the whole day without you.'

'I thought that was what you wanted,' Aisha told me with a biting smile. I ignored that.

We were in the hotel room, back after an exciting first day at the Mountain Echoes litfest. We'd walked around the city and seen most of it in two hours.

Literary superstars were overflowing onto Thimphu's high street, called Norzin Lam, from cafes and eateries. In nearby restaurants, we saw foreigners sweating from spicy *emadashi*, and a famously reclusive writer clicking selfies with the local men and women in traditional garb. I lost Tejas for about an hour when I stopped to talk to a young poet buying handicrafts.

I knew most of the people sitting on the steps by the clock tower on the lower side of Norzin Lam. I took the time to catch up with familiar faces. Publishing in India was a close-knit community. Competitive, but cooperative. It was a relaxed atmosphere, everyone was taking in the city, sitting in the sun, planning their events and going over last-minute changes. I had a bundle of business cards with me by 5 p.m. when we were to meet Pema, our local contact, at a cafe close by.

'Aisha, you wanted to rest, now let's get ready,' I said. 'Pema was so excited to see Tejas; she took us for coffee and has an awesome night planned for the three of us. You'll love her. She said we can work out a slot where I get to talk about my vision of publishing. Can you believe that? I will be addressing everyone, it's like a jumpstart to everything.'

'Yes, Ruhi almost forgot to go over my book reading's details with her,' Tejas said.

'Good for you,' Aisha muttered, sombrely looking out the window.

This wasn't her. The last time Aisha had fainted like this was at Tejas's book launch. It had been the three of us then as well. I honestly couldn't figure out what she was on about. She was in a simple white t-shirt, black pants and white trainers. The highlights in her hair caught the sun, and were in a messy bun on top of her head behind her sunglasses. Her skin was healthy, and yes her face had filled in but she looked attractive, more comfortable and healthy now – no uptightness – or maybe that was in my head. When she smiled, none of it even mattered. One of Litracy's designers was still too shy to talk to her directly. She could light up a room with her persona, yet she wasn't even grateful for it. She was caught up with something that was a figment of the past. It was hard not to be envious and a little angry.

Tejas hadn't caught on yet. And then he did. He'd picked up a sealed packet of peanuts lying on the coffee table.

'Hang on, you didn't eat anything?' Tejas said, standing in the balcony opening a new pack of cigarettes.

'I didn't feel like it,' Aisha said.

'Oh. OH,' he said.

I sat down next to Aisha, who was glaring at him.

'You have to eat something,' I told her.

'No one cares how you look, Aisha,' Tejas said, leaning inwards from the balcony, cigarette in hand.

'Easy for you to say. You don't have two thousand followers threatening to ditch you every time you gain a few grams!' Aisha said.

'Like you wouldn't believe. Smoke?' he said.

'Tejas! Don't ask her to smoke,' I said.

'Whatever makes her feel better,' he said. He put out his cigarette and went and sat down on the table opposite us. 'What will make you feel better?'

'Nothing.'

'How about more chocolate? Look at this, Tejas got the whole thing,' I said, pushing a giant Dairy Milk towards her.

'Aisha. I have fans too. You can't give in to what they think. Who are they to decide what you put in your body?' Tejas said. 'Why do you give them that power?'

'It's not just them, it's everything,' Aisha said. 'Nobody pays attention to me anymore. Or looks at me.'

'That's just not true. Ruhi, tell her, doesn't she look better now? With a bit of meat on your bones, you have more energy and are a lot more fun than before. 'Coz we can eat out and drink with you. Nothing else matters, right?' Tejas said.

'Totally, Aisha. People are in awe of you, not your body weight. Pema is dying to meet you. Even Farah thinks well of you. And she hates *everyone*.'

'I haven't faced my friends in two months,' Aisha said.

'We shouldn't have to tell you this, but if they're the kind who'll judge you for taking care of yourself, they're no friends of yours,' Tejas said.

'And what do you think we are?' I said. 'Your fans? We haven't unliked you on Facebook or stopped talking to you for such a silly little thing.'

'It's not a silly little thing, Ruhi,' Aisha said, her eyes burning through me. 'We all have our sore spots.'

Tejas put his hand on my shoulder. 'We're here to enjoy the litfest and promote Litracy,' he said. 'And as a proud parent of a book, I declare: there is no better way to do that than to get out there and get drunk.'

'You guys go ahead,' Aisha said. 'I'm fine here.'

'Hey. It is tough for you. No one is denying that. Why don't you take the good with the bad and come out with us anyway,' I said.

'The good with the bad,' Aisha repeated. 'I've heard that before I think.'

'And you can shop, buy something new! And we'll take pictures of you in it,' I added. 'Get a *kira*!'

'Sure thing,' Tejas said. 'You aren't gonna sit here and not eat all weekend, are you? You won't be starving yourself to death, we all know that. We're slaying this demon right now.' He picked up the phone, calling room service. 'Club sandwich? Chicken. Three please.'

'I'm sorry I keep doing this to you guys,' Aisha said.

'No need to apologise. Just eat,' I said.

'And eat more. And then a little,' Tejas said.

'I'm only coming because I have a lot of posts lined up,' Aisha said, breaking a piece of the chocolate.

'And not because you're here for me,' Tejas said.

'Your book. Not you,' Aisha said.

Tejas lit another cigarette.

'Only you could go to a book festival and come back with a chocolate,' Aisha said.

'What can I say. It's my drug of choice here,' Tejas said. 'I'm nervous too.'

⁓

Friday, 25 August

To Do:
• *Make notes for own speech*

• *Make the decision*

'How many books have you brought along?' Aisha asked me, piling all five on my nightstand.

They were comfort reading: Harry Potter, Jeffrey Archer, some poetry, PG Wodehouse and a Murakami.

'And a Kindle?'

'You never know where and when a bit of time will free up.' I looked at Aisha's reading for the weekend – just the magazine she'd taken from the flight.

I zipped up my bag before Aisha spotted Tejas's journal peeping out. I'd found it in the office and nicked it. It was the first time I had ever done anything like this.

Tejas had been reticent all day, behaving professionally, too professionally, like there was some distance between us. Good thing I had other things to think about and keep my mood light. I could always browse through his journal later to find out what was in his head. And there were always other things I could do to get close.

'You wouldn't be able to read all of this even if you stayed in the hotel room all weekend.'

'What about your extensive makeup collection?' I pointed at her two vanity kits. 'You have as much makeup as you do clothes.'

'That's different. I use it everyday, sometimes twice a day. And it's not just for me, but for both of us and my blog.'

'There, all done.'

I'd hung all our formals and organised the rest of the clothes according to sets. I also put the lingerie in drawers and lined up our shoes according to event.

'Wow Ruhi, you should become a professional cupboard organiser. You know they have them in Japan, people who teach how to keep stuff in drawers and the like.'

'It calms me.'

'I'm done with the toilet kits,' Aisha said.

'But you haven't even opened them.'

'Let's not waste time. We have toothbrushes from the hotel and we'll do the rest as we go along. Besides, I wanted to talk to you about something.'

'What? About Tejas?'

'Yes.'

'I was going to tell you, I'm thinking of going ahead with it. The deed.'

I pointed at the lingerie set I'd bought the day I went out shopping with her. 'And I'll need the thing you were giving me at that shop.'

'It's too soon. I don't think you're ready.'

'Maybe I am.'

'Ruhi, is it possible that this may not be the right time for you to do what you're thinking? Plus now that he's here, all his and your emotions will be riled up with his event and it may not be the best time for you to be intimate.'

'I don't know when I'll be away from my mother again. You said you were on my side.'

'I am.' Aisha put her arm around me. 'And this isn't about your mother, it's about you. You know me, I know guys and my instinct says this isn't the right time, and maybe isn't even the right person for you, Ruhi. But if you think this is what you really want, then you shouldn't listen to me. It shouldn't matter what I'm saying and it shouldn't make you this upset.'

'I'm not upset, I'm just ... all this is very new for me. I won't know how to do anything. I had to google what to do. How to put on a you-know-what. Everyone's first time is emotional, right?'

'Not in the way you think,' Aisha sighed. 'They're in the little pink pouch with the sanitary pads.'

I went to the loo, opened the pouch but closed it. It was all too freaky.

'I don't remember what I was wearing the time I lost it.' Aisha was looking at the pearly white bra and panty set, still in its packaging. 'It won't be that bad, Ruhi, and not amazing either. But, just go with the flow.'

'How old were you?'

'A lady doesn't kiss and tell.'

'Ha! Some lady.'

'Who's being catty now? And I won't be looking like a lady this weekend. All I have are tight bras. I didn't end up buying new ones. And you are so not wearing that.'

She was pointing at my black shirt and black pants.

'You told me to buy the blouse.'

'For office, in Delhi. Not this place. And certainly not dinner. Here, I'd kept this just in case.' She gave me a light-pink full-sleeved tunic dress I'd just hung.

'Pink?'

'It has a slit down the middle. Wear pants and take a shawl. Show me your shoes.'

I had a pair of sensible gold sandals. Flats.

'Gladiators, perfect.'

'What will you wear?'

'I have a black dress that looks better on me than this one.'

I guess she meant it fit better.

'For what it's worth, I think you look as good as ever.'

'I wish I felt that way,' she sighed. 'What are you wearing tomorrow?'

'I thought of the fuchsia blouse and the same pants.'

'I'll give you a skirt.'

'Okay, let's go then.'

It was around four in the afternoon and for two hours we were walking around the city clicking pictures of Aisha posing. Tejas and I had already walked through the area in the afternoon. Aisha's mood had changed dramatically.

When we got back to the hotel, I took three sachets from Aisha's pouch without telling her. I wasn't certain what would happen and I knew I was overcompensating, but who could predict these things.

We had an hour to go before leaving for dinner and I dozed off.

By the time Aisha woke me up, I had twenty minutes to get ready. She wanted me to get some rest, she said. Not the ideal situation but it couldn't be helped. I wasn't used to taking long to dress up anyway. Aisha insisted on me wearing makeup and was done with my face in ten minutes. She was looking glamorous in a black off-shoulder dress and I wasn't looking too bad in Aisha's pink tunic. Tejas was looking as good as ever, in an open collar two-piece suit.

The restaurant was in Hotel Druk and we took a cab. Our evening began with Pema having us try the local beer in the bar adjoining the restaurant. The bar was colonial in style with exquisitely carved wooden furniture and interiors, the perfect place to have a whiskey and a cigar. Tejas was thoroughly impressed.

The plan was to have dinner and then go to a karaoke bar to end the night. Pema looked completely different, about ten years younger. She was wearing a silk blouse and a trendy grey coat that reached her ankles.

After an hour into the meal, when we'd had a lot of beer and the conversation was flowing, Pema was keen to know what working at Litracy was like. I was happy to tell her the nitty-gritties. Aisha couldn't stop raving about the food and I kept a close eye on her. By the time we'd eaten our main courses, I'd lost count of how many drinks we'd had. It was good, liquid courage for me for the night to come.

Pema spent the latter of the evening gushing over Tejas and talking to him about her own travels. She was the nicest person ever but I couldn't stand their connection, to be honest.

After dinner, we went to a funky-looking karaoke bar and Tejas and her singing duets there was just too much for me to handle. I decided to leave, saying I had some planning to do.

Pema and Aisha were going to continue with the night. I'd spilled beer on myself at some point in the night but Aisha waved it off saying she'd seen worse. I didn't expect Tejas to come along but he did. I made my decision that second, when Tejas and I headed back to the hotel together.

'Wanna have a drink?' I asked when we reached the
hotel. I half-hoped he'd say no.

'Sure,' he said.

Shit.

10

Under Pressure

– TEJAS –

Friday, 25 August

All the beer has taken the edge off. I know Pema now, and Ruhi's going to be there too. I'm not that nervous about speaking tomorrow. If only that were the case with Ruhi. I can't believe I'm going to end it. It is the right thing to do. Of course, it will be painful, more for her than me. Anyway, I'll worry about that back home in Delhi.

It was good to see Ruhi having fun, but she was stumbling a bit and I decided to accompany her back to the hotel. I was enjoying her company, and decided to have one last drink with her before plying her with a full litre of water and putting her to bed. It was only 11 p.m. and she'd be good for the morning.

She really was a different person away from Farah. She spent all day wanting to kiss in public like the other tourists. I was a little wary because of what I'd decided to do, but it was okay that we could have our last dance in Bhutan.

'Hey.' She was back.

'You changed.'

Ruhi was wearing a bathrobe.

'Yes.' She came up to me and began kissing me with fresh vigour. Her hands – uh oh.

'Ruhi, we need to talk!' I said, pushing her away.

'Can't we just, you know?'

'I'm not going to, till you're sober.'

'I'm prepared.' She showed me what was in her hand.

I would kick myself for doing this while Ruhi was in such a drunk state, but I could not lead this girl on.

'Look, we can talk. But this isn't working out between us.' I told her how, when we met, she got me out of a dark spot, and I was grateful and vulnerable, but no more. Not till she was emotionally ready.

She began crying and babbling and did not stop. I listened. I went to the minibar and poured a vodka for myself. Then a rum. Despite my protests, Ruhi insisted on doing the same. I listened some more.

'Is there something wrong with me? I'll do anything for you,' she said.

'That's exactly it. I don't want a girl who'll do anything for me. Nobody does. Even you won't want a guy who'll do anything for you. Transition from the little girl you are, to the woman you can be.'

'I'll have a whiskey now,' Ruhi said.

'Sure,' I said, pouring Coke in a glass.

'It's just ... you need to find yourself first, not be in other people's shadows,' I told her, sitting down next to her.

'You mean, the shadow I'm behind – Aisha's?'

I was making it worse. 'You are your own person, and that's awesome, the best thing about you.'

'I can have another whiskey, lemme make it...'

'No.' I quickly poured the whiskey down the sink before she got to it, but she'd passed out by then.

⁓

Ruhi woke me up by splashing water on my face.

'Good morning, sunshine,' I said, though she looked like hell.

'You have an hour to leave.' She went back under the covers.

'What about you?'

'I'm not coming,' she said.

'Ruhi, we're in this together. I'm here because of you. We've come so far. Let's not spoil your hard work.'

'Don't talk to me ever again, you freak.'

'We're in this together,' I said. 'I need your support.'

'Now you need my support? You be an adult now. I'm hungover. Stop talking and leave.' Ouch. I deserved that.

I knocked on Aisha's door.

She was wearing a thin, blue dress which had a wide berth for cleavage.

'Where's Ruhi?'

'She'll come later.'

'Oh. Oh! I hope you didn't run out of … umm … anything you may have needed last night.'

'It's hot,' I fibbed. 'Let's go.' I was sweating around my neck.

She gave me a hard stare all the way till we were in the cab, without saying a word. Was she checking me out or did she want to know what happened?

'What's the schedule?' I asked.

'You know the schedule.'

'What are you going to do for social media today?'

'I've had a live Twitter feed going since we got here. I've been updating your Facebook page and putting teasers on this event page. All your fans know what you ate for dinner last night.'

'I don't think I'm up for making the speech,' I said when we got off the cab at the Royal University of Bhutan, where most of the talks happened.

'Hey. These people love you.'

Pema was waiting for us outside the auditorium with a line of about fifty people who began cheering when they saw me. We cut the line and entered the auditorium and watched the ending of an incredible performance of the *Dramtse Nga Cham*, a sacred dance of the drums with masked dancers. The audience, which was a mix of Indians, Americans, Europeans and students from Bhutan, filled in to watch Ruskin Bond talking about his life and loves. This calmed me a bit, but I dragged Aisha out of the auditorium before it was over.

'I wish Ruhi was here.'

'What?' Aisha said. 'Did something happen between you two, like a fight?'

'No I ... I don't want to do this. I'll mess up.'

'Okay. Okay. Let's just get there first.'

Aisha pushed through to the front of the audience and got Pema back with her. They had a quick conversation and Pema nodded. We followed her and got into a cab.

'Tarayana Centre,' she told the cab driver.

'Hang on,' I said.

'Tejas, trust me. The centre where your talk is happening is tiny. There will be one-fourth the number of people who were there at the last talk. Let's just go see it, okay?'

We reached the venue. My books were on display in the makeshift shop at the university campus. I had signed some copies but was to sign the ones fans brought with them.

Pema began briefing me on how to greet my fans, how much time to spend talking to them. A lot of buzz had been created through Facebook. They were expecting a good crowd.

There were thirty people and more coming in. My hands were sweaty and my heart thudded.

Aisha led me to the table where I was to sit.

'Tejas, you have to do this, you have to learn to address crowds, okay? I'll have it capped, okay? Say for safety reasons or something. Can you handle that? Only sixty people, okay? That's half the people who were there at your launch.'

'Yes. Yes, that works. I think.'

'Here, go through your notes. We'll stick to the basics today.'

Some fans had lined up early and Aisha let them come to me for the signing. I relaxed after a while. It was like talking to any other people. Some of them, especially the girls, wanted to have pictures clicked with me.

Aisha joined me when I snuck out for a clandestine smoking break. Girls outside were pointing and giggling.

'Fine now?'

'Thanks.'

'I told Pema you're the kind of author who believes in brevity, one who prefers writing over talking. Just pull her into any conversation that gets too much for you. And agree to pose questions to Mayank if you want him to talk more. It is a conversation. You're going to be great.'

'Someone wants to see you,' Aisha said giving us space to talk. Ruhi was standing behind her on the street, looking sharp in a skirt I'd never seen before.

'I had to see you,' she said.

'I was going to come see you afterwards,' I said.

'Why?'

'Given how we split up, I wanted to know if—'

'Tejas, you've made your decision and I respect it. That must have been hard for you.'

'Yes. But is it enough?'

'Not even a little bit. Good luck,' she said and turned.

'Ruhi ...' I called out.

'Tejas,' Aisha called from a distance, pointing at her watch.

Mayank Austen Soofi and Pema were ready and sitting on the couches. I took my place and got ready for a mic check. I kept my focus on the two people on stage and Aisha in the wings and took a deep breath. We were introducing ourselves. I cleared my throat and began talking.

Some sixty minutes later, Aisha was beaming at me.

'You were flawless.'

'Thank you,' I told Aisha over lunch. 'For both the things. The crowd control, and most of all, for calming me.'

'You're welcome. There was no crowd control. I made that up.' She smiled. 'Look, Ruhi's on stage.'

Her crowd was much bigger than mine. She waved to us and gestured for us to come sit up ahead.

She looked so young at that moment in her formal pink blouse and tiny skirt – a little girl trying to look like an adult. Not to mention, nursing a hangover and dealing with a breakup. What had I been thinking, doing that last night?

I was so raw and heartbroken when I met Ruhi. All of twenty-three and here was Ruhi, taking on the world while falling apart. I was a dick.

11

Finesse

– AISHA –

Saturday, 26 August

What's on your mind?

What a day for Litracy! Fantastic sessions on the Mountain Echoes stage by Managing Editor @RuhiSingh & fiction author @TejasSahni, doing what they do best. Check out @TheLiterateWhiteDog – Litracy Books's official blog for more deets. #MountainEchoes #Bhutan

Ruhi looked more upset than I'd ever seen her. We were back at the hotel and she'd filled me in on the details of last night.

'Are you sure you don't wanna come? Or I could stay,' I asked her. 'You seemed to be handling it well today.'

'No, you carry on. I'll just read and sleep.'

'You know how you feel right now, it would have been worse if you had continued dating him. You have to find a way to get back on top, otherwise every guy will make you feel this way.'

'Go away. Let me be.'

'You don't need to bend over backwards to please anyone. You have to love yourself first. Only then are you worth loving. Do you understand? Even Tejas gets that.'

She put her head under the blanket. I sat on my bed. It was only 9.30 p.m., my last night here. I could not leave her like this. I couldn't stay either.

'Ruhi, you were so "yourself" on the stage out there today, everyone could see it and they loved it.'

No response. I switched on the TV and put on a film. I ordered her a plate of pasta – she hadn't eaten much all day.

'Read your books if they'll take your mind off things.'

She didn't say anything.

'I'll be back in two hours. Call me if you need anything.'

I was to meet Tejas and Pema at the pub called Mojo Park near the city centre. They'd reach there directly.

It took the taxi ten minutes to drop me outside. The scene reminded me of a night in Hauz Khas. Live music thumped from the doorways whenever someone stepped out. Throngs of trendily dressed people were sitting around bonfires, smoking and laughing. I spotted Tejas.

'Pema got caught up with the fest and won't make it. It's going to be just us.'

'Oh great.'

'Where's Ruhi?' he said.

'You could have told her you were tired that night,' I told him point-blank. 'There's no excuse for what you did.'

'No.'

'In a way, things are good,' Tejas said, finding a cozy spot near a bonfire. 'Now Ruhi will have to learn to take care of herself, figure out what she really wants.'

'Don't,' I said, avoiding looking at him, gazing at the road to hail a cab. 'This is not a happy ending.'

'I know. I'm not trying to … I know she wasn't ready, physically. I should have known she wasn't ready emotionally either. I'm an ass.'

I didn't want to have this conversation but there were no cabs around. I sat down with him.

'I'm not going to disagree. Ruhi's easy to like.'

'And love.'

'I'm sorry you guys broke up,' I said.

'Me too. I never thought … not this soon.'

Tejas's presence next to me was making me very *very* self-conscious. I looked at him and he was looking at the fire. Maybe it was all me.

'How did you start this thing with Ruhi?' I asked. 'I mean, what do you like most about her?'

'It's not about Ruhi anymore.'

'I'm going to look for a cab,' I said, standing up and walking to the road.

'Aisha,' he called out.

I pondered the question in that one word, looking at the empty road, walking further ahead and away from him. No cabs anywhere.

'I called a number. There's one on the way,' Tejas said, catching up with me.

'I see Ruhi every day at work,' I said, turning to him and making eye contact good and proper for the first time that night.

'This is about you,' he said. 'I like how we relate, I like how you are. And today, that means a lot, how you handled everything.'

I touched his shoulder. 'I appreciate you and Ruhi taking care of me yesterday. I want to make sure if this happens, it happens for the right reasons.'

'One evening is not enough?' he said.

'I don't want Ruhi to feel like—'

'Of course.'

'We'll give it time.'

'We will.'

'But it's a yes?'

'It's a maybe.'

12

I Knew You Were Trouble

– RUHI –

Sunday, 26 August

To Do:
- *Find out sales of T's books in Bhutan*
- *Check out buzz going around of my speech with Aisha and who's saying what on Twitter & connect accordingly*
- *Have edit meet with office tomorrow for September*
- *Plan Skype with Ani & Aisha and go over backlist*
- *Get in touch with cousins, to plan our yearly holiday*

'Height of vanity,' Aisha muttered.

'He's an adult,' I said. 'He can do whatever he wants.'

We had crossed security. Tejas was being accosted by a group of girls at the airport who were fans and it seemed to annoy Aisha. For some reason she went on and on about the importance of self-respect. She said it was especially required for the dignified space we now occupied in the publishing industry.

I was tired, I didn't listen. I had exhausted all reserves that felt any emotion for Tejas Sahni. Let him enjoy the spotlight, he was going to have to get used to it somehow. I only felt relief. There was no Tejas and I.

There wasn't any need now for me to hold onto Tejas's Moleskine as a memento of our relationship. I'd return it when we were home and just say I found it at the office.

'Is he always this way with fans? How do you work with him?'

'This is a good thing, Aisha. Remember how you love having fans?'

'It's my job. His is to write.'

The airport shops brightened Aisha's mood. 'Shopping brings out the best in me,' she said. 'Come, it'll cheer you up too.'

I followed Aisha into a souvenir shop. I kept an eye on her, remembering what had happened when we arrived. At least I knew she was full. She'd eaten breakfast with me and we were going to have lunch on the flight. Still, our seats were not together, so I kept urging her to come and have a bite with me.

'I need to talk,' I said, finally getting her attention away from the shops.

'Oh, of course, babe, you must be in tatters. Why didn't you say so before?'

I didn't actually feel that awful. I just wanted her to eat. We got coffees and sandwiches and sat down.

I had spent last night alone at the hotel crying, but it had become clear to me that I'd dug myself into an emotional pit. My emotions were out of control. That wasn't me. I wasn't ready. I could have avoided this drama had I been honest with myself. Aisha had known all along. She'd tried to warn me.

'I don't know what's happening in my head. He made it clear it's over. Do I fight with him, ignore him, or be friendly?' I said.

'Be yourself. I know that sounds vague but let things play out. In the meantime, you have me.'

'I know.'

                    *

Aisha was way up in the front while I was in the middle of the plane. The two girls next to me were together and did not want to switch. Aisha was sitting with a couple whom we didn't want to ask to move either.

I decided I would check on her around lunchtime.

I was about to switch off my phone's network when my screen flashed. It was a text from Aisha saying Tejas had boarded.

I craned my neck to the right but couldn't see him. All the better for it.

It was true what I said to Aisha, I did not feel anything, but also that I didn't know how to act. I had two hours to figure it out. We were still going to be working together, and some things would change.

The plane began its takeoff. I looked for something to read. Tejas's Moleskine was with me; I would give it one last perusal before saying I found it in the office.

His handwriting was a bunch of scrawls. I could only catch glimpses of phrases here and there.

...I have to play the perfect bluff ... infatuation ... stalker levels ... I don't want to come off as a tool ... besotted with the captivating creature before me drinking coffee ... Delhicious, truly...

Hang on. Delhicious was a hashtag Aisha used to describe, well, herself.

Was this ... this was about Aisha. He wanted to be with Aisha, not me, that's why he wouldn't go all the way. Was she in on this? Was that why she was so upset when he was with his gushing fans this morning?

My heart was hammering in my chest. As soon as the seatbelt sign was off, I walked to where I could see the top of Aisha's head. Our plane had three rows. She was in the middle lane with a couple on her left. On her right, sure enough, there was Tejas.

They were laughing. Tejas's arm reached across the aisle onto her shoulder.

The worst had happened.

Forget two hours, two months were not enough to prepare for this.

Whenever Aisha or Tejas came over to say hi or go to the loo, I pretended to be sleeping.

When we reached Delhi, I feigned drowsiness and spoke little. Aisha and Tejas did a superb job of acting.

They got an Uber together. I got into the car my mother sent to pick me up. I spent the journey home tearing out pages from Tejas's journal till I'd crushed each one into a little ball.

13

Closer

– TEJAS –

Wednesday, 7 September

Since I lost my journal last week, I've been writing a satire, a spoof on fairy tales. It's not a novel, but it's going really well. I never figured short stories could be my thing. This is promising stuff. I'll get Ruhi to read it at some point, when I work up the nerve to talk to her.

We were sitting in the corner of a cafe in Hauz Khas together. It had no wi-fi so Ruhi wouldn't step foot in it.

'Ruhi is wearing her old clothes everyday.'

'What's that supposed to mean?' I asked Aisha. Today she was wearing jeans a size too tight for her, but looked amazing in them. A simple t-shirt, hair open and blue jeans, yet every eye in the room was on her. I knew for some girls it took work, but for Aisha, it didn't. Not these days anyway. She was killing it at work and looks.

'It's a reflection of her mood,' she said, digging into the fries that came with my burger.

'You mean she was in a perpetual bad mood when she was with me?' I asked.

'No, it's rebellion, anger. She's telling off everybody in the office, being a Farah. I thought she was doing okay, but clearly not. She doesn't speak to anyone in the office, not even me. When are we going to speak to her, Tejas?'

'It's just been two weeks,' I said. Two weeks within which I'd started getting to know Aisha good and proper. I could be invested in this relationship. I was ninety-nine per cent sure.

'The other day I bumped into Ruhi in the loo,' Aisha said. 'She was crying, obviously. Is she still texting you?'

'Yes. Passive-aggressive.' Ruhi had been sending me cutesy, friendly messages, followed by angry ones.

'This had to happen,' Aisha said. 'One bad boy breaks your heart and you learn to deal with them for the rest of your life.'

'Who broke yours?' I asked.

'I'm the heartbreaker. Didn't you guess?' Aisha said.

We were still getting to know each other. Aisha was surprisingly reticent about her life before me. Mine was an open book. Aisha had seen and heard what happened between Ruhi and me. Hers was more of something she liked to call a past life. All I had were vague recollections of some guy named Kartik.

'I know you don't need a man. Still, talking to me is part of the game,' I urged.

'I've had flings. Nice guys. Nothing serious. Kartik was slightly serious. Amicable split,' she said, flippant about it. 'There's just one thing that's bothering me these days.'

'I'm listening,' I said.

'I've never been this fat before. She pushed away the plate of fries which she'd eaten all by herself.

'Are you serious? I didn't think you were the type to worry about that,' I said.

'I didn't either. But it is what it is,' Aisha sighed. 'And it doesn't feel good.'

'Hey, all you need is to work out a bit. Get up in the mornings, we'll go for a run. You don't need to look good, you need to feel good. Plus, I don't mind how you look, and you shouldn't either.'

'That's a horrible thing to say,' she said.

'Thanks,' I said. This was not a conversation to have with her. I got up and stretched. 'So I'm going to spend the rest of my day writing.'

'Really?' Aisha said with a mocking look.

'Truly.'

We'd kept our relationship slow but Aisha was beginning to get a clue about my major writing block. How could I write, when she had my attention all night and we were texting everyday?

I had a castle I'd started writing about. I needed characters and I'd added one based on Ruhi before. Now I added one inspired by Aisha too.

'How about sharing what you do with others?' She asked me.

'What do you mean, like teach?' I had considered it.

'Yes, eventually teach.'

'Where? Delhi University, between Dryden and Pope? That's not me. And the exam to get qualified is something else.'

'We'll figure something out for you,' Aisha said.

'And you?' I asked her. 'Will you continue with social media for Litracy?'

'I have no clue. I don't plan these things out,' she said. 'They just happen.'

'And your parents?'

'They are good with whatever. I don't want to work eight hours a day forever, Tejas. I like doing my own thing.'

I thought about what I liked doing, and the half-baked plot I'd been toying with. I didn't know anymore.

'This is for you. I found it lying around at work.'

Aisha slid across a copy of a book called *The War of Art: Break Through the Blocks and Win Your Inner Creative Battles.*

'I know you've been having trouble submitting material. This might help you.'

'I'm not having trouble with anything. It's all on my computer,' I lied.

'Oh. I don't mean to intrude. I do like the way you write. You know I loved your book.'

'It took you three months to read it,' I said.

'But I did read it. It is too, uh, intimate. Is that the correct usage of the word?'

'Yes. Intimacy. But more than that, vulnerability. That's at the heart of all good writing. Putting yourself out there. And it's not nice when someone tells you how to do your job,' I added softly. 'You know what, though? I'm sending you a short story. Do with it what you will.'

'That's great. And I get it, Tejas, okay? I won't nag you about this. It's between you and editorial.'

'Thank you.'

'And I don't mean to pry but I couldn't find any of your writing for May. Ruhi said we can quote from your journals at times.'

'I lost that Moleskine.'

'Moleskine, you mean diary? Like this one?' She picked up my leather-bound black diary.

'I saw one like this in Ruhi's bag on the trip.'

'I have a lot of writing in there. Maybe she forgot to give it to me. I'm not going anywhere near her though. You'll have to ask her for it.'

14

Delicate

– AISHA –

Sunday, 18 September

What's on your mind?

If you liked @Litracy's The Indian Detective Novel Series, wait till you catch book #3. The author Neel Rathore will be there in person to launch it with an exciting treasure hunt, bundles of fun for youngsters & those young at heart on September 24th, the coming Sunday @OxfordBookStore, Delhi. #WD #Litracy #NeelRathore

'You're spoiling me, Tejas.'

'I know.'

It was Sunday. I usually spent the day having a long soak in the tub with bath salts and a magazine followed by writing a blog post. Now I'd started going for morning runs with Tejas. All the better. I hated looking at my overflowing self in the mirror. I hardly wrote on my blog these days; my readers did not seem that interested in reading about food and fitness. All the attention went to the #metoo articles circulating these days.

Today, however, Tejas wanted to write, so I went to Lodhi Gardens without him and he asked me to meet him at his place after.

When I got there, he had a breakfast spread ready for me. There was French toast with cinnamon and strawberries, chocolate smoothies and strong filter coffee. He even had roadside-style bun-omelettes with sev and chutney.

'You've been creative, and your staff busy.'

'Yes yes, you've been looking quite emaciated lately.'

'Don't you patronize me. I'm actually fifty-eight kilos now and gaining.' I poured the coffee and took a slice of the toast.

'I hadn't noticed.'

'Don't lie to me. And this is the third breakfast you've made for me this month.'

'I'm showing you what every morning can be like,' he said, making a plate for me with bits of everything.

'This a ploy to get me to stay over?' I said, digging in.

'Maybe. How is Ruhi doing?' Tejas asked. 'Let's get he blessing and get on with things?'

'I will, I will. Tomorrow is the day. She hasn't been regu at work. Works from home mostly, and when she con she broods silently at her desk. It's like she's in depres All she says is hello to me and then back to work. At her productivity is off the charts. But, tough luck, rumour has it that Litracy is going to be absorbed into WD.'

'What do you mean?' Tejas said.

'They will run it as a letterhead, meaning only an editor or two will be assigned to it. The Litracy office might be shut down or used for HR. No separate managing editor, just an editor and assistant.'

'Man, that sucks. Litracy's made strides hasn't it?'

'Yes, but the company hasn't. It needs to downsize. Hey, have you been checking your mail lately?'

'No, you know how I am. Why?'

'Just some office stuff. Farah was asking if you have anything for us yet?'

'Can't you make do with what you've got? Post things about authors, their inspirational quotes and so on?' Tejas was skirting around the topic as usual. I didn't push it.

'I can, and I have, for social media. I think editorial anted to know. Guess Ruhi's avoiding you.'

'Tell them I'm expanding the short story.'

' like that short story.' I'd entered it in a competition. I
ht it would be a nice surprise if he won.

ow you do.'

you written anything about me?' I asked.

ou want to be my muse?'

I already was.'

ou when I'm ready. I have stuff about you,
h,' Tejas said.

that. You know, in the past few months,
to Ruhi. Mountain Echoes really turned
r.'

'Good. She tries too hard to please her mother,' I said.

'Now that I think about it, that's how it was with me. I could never know what she was really thinking. Everything was "whatever you want, whatever you say, whatever you like". All I know for sure is that she loved my writing. But then, so do most people,' Tejas said.

'You're vain and you don't even know it.' I was teasing him, but his ego was really beginning to bother me.

'I am not.'

'Why do you carry those reviews around, not to mention your book everywhere you go?' I pointed at the raggedy copy of his book with newspaper and magazine cuttings in it.

'It's for inspiration.'

'When I want inspiration, I pick up a mag, or open Pinterest and see what others are up to. New energy. You should do the same.'

'Yeah, read. I do. You have as many magazines as I do books. But in all honesty, writing a blog post is nothing compared to writing a book.'

'There you go again. Vain.'

'Let's drop it. More food?' He said, looking at my empty plate.

'No thanks.'

He was clearly struggling with his work; I didn't want to piss him off. And what he said, said more about him than me anyway. Though if he did not change his tune, I wouldn't put up with it for long.

Monday, 19 September

What's on your mind?

Listen up, history buffs! Litracy author & historian @MaliniSingh is giving a guided tour of the Hauz Khas lake and fort, which is also the setting of her gripping fictional bestseller, Once Upon a Dynasty. *Choose your dates & sign up here. #WDIndia #HKV #DelhiWalks*

I was alone in the Litracy conference room and it was almost lunchtime.

Ruhi wasn't around and the designers along with the interns had gone to try the fusion place supposed to be the new Coast Cafe. I passed, as I was going to try my luck and apply for the JLF core team on a whim. I'd met the week's deadlines and because of Ruhi's lack of teamwork at the moment, work was a little slow. Everyone loved my work at the litfest. Another one would be great exposure.

To apply, we had to write a short email to Farah about what we've done in the company and how we're going to be beneficial as part of the JLF team. Today was the last day to apply, and they were going to announce the team in the afternoon.

Maybe Ruhi was making finishing touches on her application and wanted to do that in peace at home. I hope she got it, throwing herself into work will help her move on. She has been taking random half-days throughout the month; everyone thinks she's not well, but no one wanted to ask Farah. People kept asking me and I didn't know what to say.

I finished the application and took out my salad. I didn't have a fork so I fished through Ruhi's drawer to find one, and that's when I saw it.

The spine and cover of Tejas's diary with the pages torn out. The cover was black but he'd scratched a T inside. Unmistakeable. Shit. Ruhi had had his Moleskine all along. I felt stupid, I knew how infatuated Ruhi was with him but I'd never realised the extent of her obsession.

If we both got on the JLF team, it would be the best way to help her get back to normal.

I felt it best not to tell Tejas. Let him think he misplaced his journal.

I ate lunch by myself while browsing *Harper's Bazaar* and *Marie Claire* online. The international versions were always better than the Indian ones, though I couldn't spot a single person my size on their sites. I could dare to be different. The fashion industry was infamous for perpetuating skinny culture.

I didn't even know there was a skinny culture. Unwittingly, I had been conforming to and propagating it, as Maya had explained to me. Through her encouragement, I was shifting from eating well to looking well. I was starting to enjoy different kinds of cuisine, and was having ravioli leftovers from the Italian restaurant Tejas and I had gone to last night. I had even begun skipping out on the salads recently. I vowed to change that.

By the time I finished, Ruhi entered the office. She was wearing tights and an old shirt and looked exhausted.

'Hi,' I said.

She smiled, glancing at my neck. Shoot. I pried my hair open to cover it. Damn that hickey from last night. I usually used concealer to hide them but had forgotten to today.

'Ready for the announcement?' I asked.

'Yes. Farah's getting ready to mail us.'

The rest of the office had started returning. I went back to work, sitting with Saloni and Rahul in the design section. Ruhi's presence was too gloomy to bear these days.

In hindsight, I'd sent in my application just an hour ago and no one would have had the time to read it. I forgot about it and began brainstorming ideas with Saloni.

I had devised ways of amping up each Litracy author's social profile, even if it meant posting on their behalf. The way to do that was infographics and user engagement. It was quite a bit of trend research, but taking it week by week, I was a fortnight ahead.

Next, I began working on Tejas's campaign. He was the only author who was reticent when it came to replying to emails and sending ideas for social media. Then again, he was the only one who was twenty-six and living it up. Maybe I was just prejudiced towards him. I checked the list of his favourite authors. How much of Kerouac and Bukowski could I add to his page? It's not as if he made things easy for me by telling me what he read. I had to fish around his house.

'Aisha, what are you doing?' Saloni said. 'I have a message from Farah, saying you have to join in on a con-call right now.'

'Oh, I was just focusing on this—'

'The JLF Planning Committee is meeting right now.'

'Oh, so?'

'Well, get in on the call, you don't want to give the others a bad first impression, do you?'

'I got in. I got in.' I grabbed my earphones and headed back to the conference room where Ruhi was.

'We're on! Ruhi, I'm in as well, can you believe it? We're gonna have the best time,' I said to her, logging onto Skype. 'Wanna join in?'

'No,' she said, taking her laptop and going and sitting outside on a beanbag.

Oh well. I'd speak to her after the meeting. I couldn't stop smiling. This would look excellent on my resume. This was actually something to boast of. Wouldn't my followers love to know.

I was on video conference with the Gurgaon office. The WD Asia CEO, Mr. Desai, was present as well. Stocky and gray, he looked like the kind of man who owned a company. Everybody else was dressed casually enough. Farah introduced me to Harsh, from Marketing, Adit the designer and Sumit from Production, each heads of their respective departments.

'Where's Ruhi?' I asked her, expecting her to be joining in on another computer, but she shushed me.

'Aisha, right? Welcome to the team,' Mr. Desai said. 'We're deciding on a website. Here is our vision,' he continued, explaining exactly what the website should offer. 'You can come to Gurgaon a couple of times a week?'

'Of course, sir.'

'Keeping that in mind,' Adit said. 'What do you think?'

'Okay, let's start with the static layout, what visitors see when they land on the site for the first time.'

⁓

I was the first to find out when the #metoo news broke all over the internet but the last to find out that Ruhi hadn't made the team. I found Ruhi in the cafe sitting with a black coffee, Ani with her green tea. Ani hadn't applied to JLF; there was different a PR for that purpose. Both of them would have their days and nights turned upside down now. They had no idea of the mess that Litracy was going to have to handle.

'I'm so sorry,' I said. 'Ruhi, we need to talk. Something big has happened.'

Ruhi turned her face away. Her eyes were red.

'Ruhi, can you talk to me for five minutes?'

'Ruhi does not want to talk to you right now,' Ani said.

'I'm not talking to you, Ani. You should get upstairs urgently. Something about some author badmouthing the non-fiction managing editor on TV, #metoo.'

'You're lying,' she said.

'Only one way to find out,' I told her.

'Ruhi, I'll be right back. Don't let her get to you,' Ani said, checking her phone.

'Fuck, fuck, fuck, Aisha this is bad.'

'You'd better get on it,' I said as Ani ran upstairs.

'You weren't even gonna apply for JLF, Aisha,' Ruhi said, banging her hand on the table.

'Ruhi, something big is going down. I just wanted to see how you were.'

'You're the one who stole Tejas from me.'

I had to sit down. *Shit.* I took a deep breath.

'Ruhi, you knew? Since when? I was going to tell you. Nothing *really* happened.'

'It's all the same to you, isn't it? Stepping on whoever is between you and what you want.'

'That's not true. You and Tejas are some of the closest friends I've ever had.'

'I don't care, Aisha. If I mean anything to you, you will give me your position in the JLF core team.'

'I'm sure you can help out. I'll ask Farah. Let's try and work through this,' I told her. 'I'm sure you can be valuable right now.'

'I am not going to help out. I want to lead.'

'We don't have time for this, Ruhi.'

'I should have been the one sitting in on the call today,' she said forcefully.

'Oh God, fine. I don't know what to tell you, they want advice on social media, they need my expertise. Maybe it's not about me over you at all.'

'It's social media. It's not rocket science. I was doing it before you got here, Aisha. I did not even have to run spell check before posting anything, like you have to.'

'You know what, Ruhi? You're being a bitch now. If you deserved the position, you would have got it. And I'll tell you another thing, I would have been assigned to the JLF team even if I hadn't applied, Farah told me so in confidence. I'm good at what I do and I'm not apologising for that.'

'I think you must have planned everything that happened in Bhutan. Tejas was supposed to be with me. You took over *my* job, got on his good side and screwed me over.'

'Ruhi, you were hungover. I didn't pour the alcohol down your throat. And he'd already broken up with you then, remember?'

'You told me not to sleep with him. You wanted him for yourself, that's why you told me not to.' Ruhi was standing up now. People in the cafe were beginning to stare.

'Shut up, Ruhi.'

'How come you're dating him then?'

'He actually likes me,' I said.

'Why are you doing this to me?'

'I'm not doing anything to you. Don't be a victim. You're an adult. There are more fish in the sea.'

'I think maybe you even started dating him when we were going out. Before Bhutan.'

'Ruhi! We're your friends. You're just imagining the worst in your head. None of it is true.'

'I'm not stupid, even though I know you both think I am. I thought I wasn't good enough for Tejas.'

'You can't depend on him to make you feel good about anything, Ruhi!'

'You're the most unreliable person I know. I have done nothing but help you from the very beginning, when you passed out at Tejas's book launch.'

'I fainted! You assumed that just because I was wearing a short dress and heels, I had passed out drunk, half an hour into a work party? You don't know anything about me. What if it had been you? I would have thought twice before judging you.'

'Aisha, I left a book launch of my publishing house to help you. I was following my instinct. *You* don't know how to be a friend, let alone recognise one. You're a machine, you'll have followers for sure, never people in your life that actually matter.'

'It's not my fault Tejas does not like you anymore; we got together after you guys split up. It's not my fault your mother doesn't take you seriously. You haven't taken responsibility for anything in your life. In fact, you're blaming me, blaming your mother, blaming Tejas. Fact is, nobody would know you existed if she hadn't given you this chance. Use, don't abuse, what you have.'

Ani was back. 'Farah wants us *now*,' she yelled over my voice. 'Aisha was right. White Dog is screwed.'

15

Bitch

– RUHI –

Monday, 1 October

To Do:
- *Email Aisha asking for social media figures*
- *Ask Ani market potential and promotion strategy for steampunk novel*
- *Induct interns on Skype*
- *Write appraisal email*

I was in the office loo wiping the mud off my new Adidas sneakers.

Two weeks had elapsed since #metoo had rocked Litracy's world. After the non-fiction managing editor was asked to leave, all of Litracy's resources were being used for non-fiction. I had interns but work was chaos and I didn't know what to do. I just spent time trying to coach myself through getting through everything.

I was finally getting some slack from my mother. Ever since I'd returned from Thimphu, she was in awe of my speech. I was going through an upheaval emotionally but she figured I had too much on my plate. That was her reason for not having me on the JLF team. I couldn't catch a break. She even wanted me away from the whole #metoo nonsense.

She'd also dropped a bomb telling me that while I had been great at my role, Litracy's days were coming to an end.

Aisha was in the loo with me. I confused her with an intern for a second and said hi. She'd caught the rain on her white blazer and was shaking off the water. She was wearing a black blouse and jeans, but I could see the weight around her belly.

'Hi Ruhi,' she said, staring at my hair.

'I did it myself. What do you think?' I'd taken a pair of scissors over the weekend and given myself a haircut. It's not something I would do on my own but the situation warranted it. I was done with looking at the same tired face. My long hair was gone and I had a shoulder-length messy blunt cut instead. I looked younger and older at the same time. I put on a fresh coat of lipstick, I'd invested in my own. I tucked my white blouse into my jeans, turning enough times to make sure Aisha noticed my waist. I'd always been waif-like.

'Here,' I offered her the lipstick. It was light pink, too subtle for her style, but she took it.

'Thanks. Too much work. Don't ask,' Aisha said. 'I don't know where my stuff is. All this shuffling between here and Gurgaon is crazy.'

Between her place and Tejas's is what she really meant, I guessed. *Bitch.*

All she spoke about to anyone in the office was *Tejas this* and *Tejas that*, smiling and flaunting her love bites. Anyone would guess something was up. Now that she was too busy to have a minute to spare, it was easier for me to ignore her.

Though I was doing just the opposite at the moment. Aisha was too worked up with her Litracy and JLF workload to care about what she was eating. I had been ordering in from all the places I could think of, asking Aisha what she'd have. She thought I was opening my heart to her, while I was picking out the unhealthiest things on the menu.

'KFC today?' I asked her when we were back in the edit room.

'Sure.'

Some evenings I'd even noticed her take leftovers back home. How did Tejas feel about that, I wondered. He liked well-put-together women, not haphazard messes. The princess was turning into a frog. She deserved it. I trusted her with all my heart and she'd destroyed me.

I did not show it, but a storm was brewing under the surface.

Thank god for Ani, who heard me out whenever I needed to talk. She also reported on Aisha for me, taking frequent smoking breaks with her and coming back to me with gossip.

'Hey, Aisha, I've been sharing your blog on Facebook. I know there hasn't been that much traffic there lately.'

'Thanks, Ruhi.'

Aisha was completely distracted from real life. A month ago, she would have told me off for making a comment like that in front of anyone.

'I'm looking for the editor, Ruhi.' An intern was at the door. I signalled him in. He had manuscripts with him, which he put in front of Aisha.

'Those are for me,' I said.

'They're for the editor. Aren't you the social media manager?'

'I am,' Aisha said after a second, then walked out with her pack of cigarettes. I recognised the look on her face. It was one I often saw in myself.

'What did I do?' he said.

'Nothing. Thank you so much for these.'

He blushed. 'Anything else I can do for you?'

'Yes. Come with me.' I went for a walk, taking my time walking across the floor and down to the cafe. The interns loved staring at the girls walking by and they gave the boy following me a thumbs-up. Yup. Was I the new Aisha?

I got myself an iced tea and a regular Coke for Aisha. Out of the kindness of my heart. The intern carried the drinks to my desk.

I took the Coke out and handed it to Aisha by the smoking area.

'For you. Diet.'

Aisha smiled at me. 'I'm glad we're talking again.'

According to Ani, Aisha was totally incapable of handling all the work stress and was taking it out on Tejas. Now that I happened to know there was smoke in paradise, all I had to do was light a fire.

'Me too,' I smiled. 'Without the hashtag.'

16

Tainted Love

– TEJAS –

Saturday, 15 October

The reason I feel scared to write is because I know there's a part of me that I'm putting out there, it's like your child that you put out in the world which you already know to be a confusing place. I'm open and vulnerable to criticism about the people I put into my stories, their thoughts, their actions, their lives.

What will you say, when you begin to understand that I have fallen out of love?

Aisha was languidly lying on the sofa in my bedroom. What a few months ago would have had me on my knees in a second, made me want to break something.

'I can't stand this, Aisha.'

'You don't stand up for my needs,' Aisha muttered, eyes closed, not even looking at me.

'You don't stand for anything. I'm not attracted to somebody begging me to tell them how much I like their body.'

'But you used to like it before.'

'*You* used to love it before,' I said, grabbing my cigarettes and heading to the garden. As her house was littered with delivery and takeout boxes, I'd suggested I'd fix her dinner at my place this weekend.

We'd been dating for more than a month and we hardly saw each other.

'Tejas,' she came out and sat down next to me. 'What's your worst fear?'

'Not being able to write I guess.'

'Mine is losing confidence in myself – and it's coming true.'

Mine was coming true as well. But I didn't say it.

'People are insulting me on my blog daily, Tejas. It's the reason, I have everything I have today. It's a lot for a twenty-something to accomplish, and worse when it's under jeopardy.'

'People are pricks. You have to stop thinking about what they say. Fuck everything. You have to take care of yourself. You're stressed out. Let's go for a run.'

'I'm not fat. You don't think my body is good enough, do you?'

'I didn't say that.'

'Oh man. I know I should be exercising, but there is just so much work to do for JLF. I feel ugly. I look ugly. People don't check me out like they used to. Random guys have stopped flirting with me.'

'Sounds like a lot of unnecessary waste of time is done with.'

'Not for me.'

'Maybe there is more to life than being the most attractive person in the room? Maybe now is the time to find it?' I said.

'Hm.' She looked up at me.

'When I began liking you, it was your attitude I adored. Life was a breeze for you. What didn't work wasn't even in your periphery. You have to discover that part of you again. What happened to "feeling good is looking good"? What feels good to you?'

'Someone mistook me for Ruhi yesterday. I'm the hot one, or I used to be.'

'She's your friend.'

'She's pretending to be. Making me eat junk food all the time. I see through her.'

'I'm sure part of her still cares.'

'Yeah, at least she's talking to me, but you weren't there when we fought.'

'Let her process things however she wants.'

'It's been six weeks! Anyway, Ruhi is the least of my concerns. I'm going crazy, Tejas. I can't say no to food. This isn't me.'

'I get that it's hard. Look, let's go for a walk. Clear your head and I'll cook you the most delicious, healthy meal you've ever had, okay?'

'I have to work now.'

꩜

I was getting annoyed with Aisha and her touch-me-not attitude. It had been weeks since we'd spent a weekend together and done anything besides sleep. It was clear that she didn't want to be alone, but she was refusing to spend time talking or even sitting with me and ignored the meals I'd been cooking for her.

I've supported Aisha in every way I could think of. If she was working on weekends and skipped a meal, if I was around I put together a healthy one. I had smoothies and salads delivered to her Gurgaon office, or would take her for dinners after work. I gently pointed out when she was smoking too much. I even made a diet chart because she didn't have the time to go meet her nutritionist. My patience was running out now.

I was watching a movie in the bedroom and she was working in the next room. This is what our weekends had turned into. Us in different rooms in her house or mine.

'Tejas, check your mail,' Aisha yelled.

'You wanna watch *Top Gun* with me?' I asked her. I was taking a break from all the crap I ended up writing these days and it was just the movie to break my rut.

'Not today. Reply to the mail, Tejas.'

'I will.' It must be about JLF. Litracy was trying to put me on a panel to talk about my next book and I had to come up with a valid excuse to avoid it.

Aisha entered the room.

'Come join me, it's the weekend,' I told her.

'It's been half an hour. We're waiting for your reply.'

'To the mail? I haven't seen it yet.'

'I told you to.'

'It's a Saturday night.'

'Farah's working and so am I.'

'No one will mind. Take a break, it's the weekend. What if you burn out?'

'Stop telling me that. I need a list of possible things you can talk about as a panel member ASAP. I'm trying to get Karan Bajaj on the same panel.'

'I'm not doing that. And that's not even your job. Why are you giving yourself extra work?'

'I have a life, Tejas. Ambitions. Dreams. Goals. I don't just sit and watch movies all day.'

'Hey. Whatever happened to not working eight hours a day forever?'

'Expert deflection, Tejas. I forgot who I was talking to. Forget the panel thing. Just give me more things to put online,' Aisha said.

'What is that supposed to mean? I'm not deflecting anything.'

'You think I'm stupid? I know you haven't written anything since you gave your final draft of *Carnival* to Ruhi eight months ago. I have a good mind to tell Farah you have nothing to show for a book that's supposed to be ready in eight weeks.'

'You know what I have. Why are you asking me? It will all work out.' I'd shown her all my many plots and told her that somewhere from those ideas is where the next book was coming from. Which was true, I just needed everything to click.

'That's not enough. Litracy isn't doing you any charity. The truth is, you don't feel your work is good enough and no one would have published it, had it not been for them. For all your arrogance, there's nothing underneath, no confidence, literally you're a nothing.'

Instead of yelling back, I just left the house for an hour and went for a run. When I got back, Aisha was sitting at the table with two glasses of wine.

'Look,' she said. 'It's not easy to maintain a website. I was covered by magazines, blogs, newspapers. There's no knowing what will work and what won't. Now look at my site, it's hard for me to even get a hundred comments a day now. I'm working very hard to make sure that doesn't happen to you. Do you hear me?'

'I do. Please understand, I'm not okay using what I have for social media, not yet. Tomorrow I'll go through my notes and figure out something. You just worry about JLF. I'll handle the rest, including Farah.'

'Good. I think I will take the night off,' she said. 'What's next for you?'

'More wine? I have this.' I held up the joint I'd been rolling.

'I mean in life. Royalties off one book can't pay off your career.'

'True,' I said. 'But we finished that conversation. Are you going to continue with your interrogation or are we going to have some fun? It's been a while.'

She turned like a whip.

'You mean sex? You couldn't be cruder.'

'I thought you were taking the night off. Aisha, what exactly do you want from me?'

'I want to see you winning at life. I'm not anymore,' she said. 'Is that a lot to ask? I'm going to go home now.'

'Fine. Go.' I lit my joint. I knew what I had to do.

17

Timepass

– AISHA –

Monday, 17 October

What's on your mind?

Volunteer for JLF! Online, onsite – the options are many. Have fantastic exposure & the experience of a lifetime. Check out this page for more info. #JLF #WDIndia #Volunteering

As usual, I didn't sleep well last night, but I was still the only one here on time at White Dog Gurgaon. I liked the polished white interiors of this huge office. There were colourful shelves with books and frames with writing quotes. The open cubicles were black and white, the colours of the White Dog logo. Usually the energy in this place, powered-up people going from one meeting to the next, was visceral. Today was an exception.

It was rainy, the kind of day you wanted to skip school for but were not allowed to. Instead, we would bunk class and drink illicit hot coffee (we were kids) in the cafeteria, and eat fried spring rolls. The classes would be half-empty with the teachers taking it easy too.

Things hadn't changed. I was outside with my coffee and I could hear frogs all around. The air was kind of cool though it was only October. I knew some people would be 'falling sick' today and nobody would mind.

Rainy days aside, it was so quiet because the office was going through appraisals. Those who were here, were gathered on the top floor getting assessed. For two days the company would be functioning in a different way. My turn would come later in the day at four, after Ruhi. I wasn't not worried.

I could have come in late but I didn't want to be alone and I didn't want to pile on Tejas either, so I came to work. I was enjoying this rare lull in work, at work.

I saw an Audi turn towards the office lane. Was it– it was Tejas. He didn't bother giving it to the valet for parking. It seemed like he was dropping by for a quick visit. Maybe to apologise.

I checked my phone; no message from him. He must have come all the way to apologise. I figured after talking to him, I could get him to talk to Ruhi, who was here too and hadn't seen him in months. They could make peace and all of that.

I went inside. He didn't see me, just entered Farah's room straight away.

I got a cappuccino refill for myself and a coffee for him, strong and black. I sipped my coffee, sitting outside the editorial room. Farah nodded at whatever Tejas was saying. She glanced at me for a second.

Did he get his head straight and want to strategise for his website? Probably.

Tejas shook hands with her. I wanted to barf. He hated these professional necessities. Then he came up to me and asked me if we could talk. Somewhere private.

'I thought you were working in Hauz Khas today,' Tejas said.

'Here I am. Coffee?' I asked as we stepped into a glass cubicle that was empty. 'What was that about?'

'Aisha, are you wearing slippers to work? I mean it's White Dog, not Litracy.'

'Oh. It's a trend that's picking up.' I hadn't noticed my slippers till I had reached the office.

'All right. So I've been thinking a lot about our conversation on Saturday and I came here to talk to Farah about it,' he said.

'Sure. Now that you're here, let's have a strategy meeting. I have time today.'

'Aisha,' he said, slowing his words down, 'I'm sorry.' He fumbled and took a deep breath. 'I'm trying to be professional. I, uh, I thought you wouldn't be here and Farah would deal with this.'

'Deal with what?'

'I see you have too much work. We aren't getting any time together, it's ruining your health and our relationship. I asked for you to be replaced.'

'What?'

'Somebody else will be handling my social media from now. It will free you up. For more important things. Like JLF. And me.'

'You mean Ruhi. She doesn't know social media in this office like I do.' I tried to stay calm and control my voice. 'She thinks google crawlers are window cleaners at Google.'

'I know you're going through a lot with your own blog losing followers and your body ... issues.'

'You mean how fat I'm getting.'

'No, and you know it. I want to be there for you and I think a little less work is going to be helpful. Just take it easy for some months.'

'Tejas, I'm being honest with you. I'm the only one in this place who knows how to get you more visibility. I know exactly how to pitch you to your readers.'

'The decision has been made.'

'Tejas, we're in this together. Look at me.'

'Let's talk about this when you're home.'

'No.'

'Don't do this here, Aisha.'

'You're the one who came here. You'd already decided. You did not even want to tell me in person.'

'I just did. Be reasonable, Aisha. You can't handle your own blog, have you seen your numbers lately? Your subscribers are dropping day by day. Why would I give you mine? You'd make the same decision in my place.'

A few people were beginning to stare. I sort of lost it right then.

'You are the one who's in this shit because you call yourself a writer and have not written a word for months. You can't handle that I know you're not worth anything. Nobody will be able to help you till you face your own demons, Tejas. Remember, you were the one to push me away. Didn't this happen with Ruhi? Whenever someone gets close to seeing what a coward you are, you hide by being a dick. I am done with you. It's over.'

Ruhi knocked and entered. She took Tejas. She said Farah wanted to see both of them immediately, and told me to take a breath and calm down. The only words she'd said to me this month.

~ ~

Ruhi gave me a hard stare when I went to my makeshift cubicle at WD. I ignored her. I did not have the time to endure whatever passive-aggressive game she was playing.

I was worried Tejas's complaint would affect my appraisal. It wouldn't, I reasoned. In four months, I had single-handedly boosted Litracy's social media and created massive followings for many authors, including Tejas.

By the time it was 4 p.m., I couldn't stop thinking about the break-up with Tejas. I wasn't going to go back on my word, but it was so painful.

Since morning I'd gone to the loo to cry innumerable times and had had enough cigarettes and coffee for my hands to shake. I couldn't think of eating and I wanted this day to be over. I hadn't had such a breakup before – one that actually hurt. Everyone I had gone out with before had been timepass.

Ruhi's appraisal was before mine and she gave me a smile as she left the room. Her empty smiles were beginning to get old, but today's gave me a shiver.

I sat down in front of Farah and an elderly female HR rep, whom I'd never seen before. I had prepped an entire speech for both of them but the rep interrupted me.

'You know we frown upon inappropriate relationships in the workplace,' she began. 'There has been a rumour going around in the office for the past few months about you and the author Tejas Sahni.'

My heart sank.

'I can clarify whatever you want me to.'

'You know what we're asking,' Farah said.

'What if somebody confirmed a relationship between you and the author?' the HR lady asked.

Shit. Ruhi had already done it. No point in lying.

'I have let nothing come in the way of my work here.'

'Can you deny the relationship?'

'No.'

Farah looked more harrowed than angry.

'It's frowned upon, not forbidden,' I added. I had a good mind to show her pictures of Ruhi and Tejas together.

'The only reason I got angry was because the author said I couldn't manage my own website, the numbers of which are dwindling, and I was not fit to work on his. I'm not responsible for the audience which fails to accept large women as storytellers. This factor simply does not reflect my work ethic.'

'You haven't seen the press release, have you?' The rep said.

'I'm sorry this is happening, Aisha,' Farah said, pushing her iPad towards me.

There I was, in a picture tagged by some unknown person on Facebook, yelling at Tejas, teary-eyed. The caption read: Office Romance Gone Wrong – Tejas Sahni, Bachelor Again.

'They even got a direct quote from him somehow,' Farah said, looking at the article with disgust.

I was speechless. I'd missed the update as I had stopped checking my social media for lack of traffic.

'You do know someone in the office put this up. Shouldn't you be more concerned who that is?' I said.

'They might have done a smart thing, getting free publicity for Tejas Sahni. It's doesn't present you in the best light on appraisal day, Aisha. Ordinarily such a frivolous thing would not matter, but this after the #metoo incident where we fired a senior editor, it gives us bad press and it puts you in a bad light. Also, you have quite a few people against you and none of your colleagues seem ready to vouch for you. Your work quality has been dropping, your health seems to be suffering as well. Additionally, this incident is grounds for dismissal as it shows how your relationship has been affecting your professional life and office decorum.'

'Your attire has been reflecting unprofessionalism too, lately,' the HR lady added, looking at my slippers.

'I've been working hard,' I said.

She ignored that. 'You don't have to serve a notice period as you are listed as a consultant on our payrolls.'

I began standing up.

'I regret this happened,' Farah said. 'Your love life makes no difference to me.'

'A break would be good. I'd get some exercise,' I said, and laughed at my own joke.

'I completely oppose you being asked to leave, Aisha. Because of your performance in the JLF meetings, I convinced Mr Desai you needed some time to yourself, because of health reasons,' Farah said. 'Email me at the beginning of next year.'

'A word about Tejas. He is not inspired. It might be a while before you can boost his digits online. Who–'

'You can leave,' the rep said.

'You can email me anytime, Aisha, for anything,' Farah said.

I nodded.

'Thank you, Farah,' I managed to croak before going back to an empty house, with nothing to look forward to in life.

18

Bored Games

– RUHI –

Monday, 17 October

To Do:
- *Hound T for novel*
- *Scout blogs and Facebook groups for promising new writers*

'It turned out better than I had imagined.' I was looking at the bulletin with the picture that Ani had tagged Aisha's social media handles on. She'd made a fake account and shared it through Facebook, Instagram and Twitter.

'Pity they aren't going to do a print story about it,' Ani said. 'People are talking about it non-stop.'

'They broke up. I know that for sure,' I told her. 'And her appraisal wouldn't have gone well thanks to the story.'

'You're going to get the JLF gig now. They won't have somebody as unprofessional as Aisha on it.'

By the time I reached the edit room, I had about fifty mails I was marked on. I found Farah there alone. Aisha wasn't around for me to gloat at.

'I'm sure you haven't heard,' she began in her saccharine yet sarcastic tone she used when she was annoyed with me but had no real reason to be so.

'A lot happened while you were on your break. We had to ask Aisha to leave and have assigned her JLF slot to you. And her clients as well. I'm sorry about it but you just have to work through it.'

'She's been let go?'

'Suspended till next year,' her voice softened. 'We should have consulted you, Ruhi, you being the managing editor at Litracy and as she was hired by you, but we were doing the appraisals and I couldn't arm-twist HR. I did what I could to keep her on the payroll. Her loss is your gain. I know you wanted the position.'

I didn't intend for Aisha to get fired, just kicked off JLF.

'Tejas had to leave. He can meet you at six, he said. Fix up a place. He's the only one you need to see in person about social media. Don't waste time making new content, tell him to email you a short story synopsis or teaser or poem. Get him to agree on whatever you want to publish online today. Look at all of Aisha's clients and her spreadsheet today. She's quite organised so you won't have to worry about social media till next week. I want you to focus on catching up with JLF till then. After that, just spend a day, a few hours a week, scheduling social media.'

'Got it.'

'And since you're friends, sometime this month go meet Aisha and show her your plan.'

'Meet her?'

'Yes, she had some valuable inputs about the panels, I'd hate for them not to be implemented. I'm sure she wouldn't mind.'

'Oh.'

'And another thing. I need Tejas's novel. Whatever he has. Even if it's a few chapters. Aisha mentioned he's having trouble with it. Give him two weeks.'

'Sure.'

I sat and gathered my thoughts. Aisha was fired. She would not be coming to Litracy or WD any longer. Because of me. I wouldn't have to see her face across my desk any longer. And I was on the JLF committee.

I opened my mailbox and grinned at my reflection on the computer screen. I had changed a horrible situation I was in and made it work for myself. I pulled my hair into a bun and called for a coffee. I had to be alert for the next three months. It was the beginning of my future and the rest of my life. Now that I knew I had power, nothing was ever going to be the same.

～

I met Tejas at his favourite coffee shop in Khan Market. The cafe was within a bookshop. They still displayed copies of Tejas's novel, and he loved going there. This was going to be the first proper conversation I'd have with him since that night in the hotel in Thimphu. At least it was a casual setup. I told myself to meet him like any other author.

I was nervous, but I don't think he could tell.

'One salted caramel cappuccino and an Americano for me,' Tejas told the barista and we sat down.

'Why'd you bring work with you?' Tejas asked.

'You haven't heard. Litracy had to let Aisha go.'

'Because of me?'

'Your fight ended up appearing on Twitter. And it was appraisals day. Farah had no choice.' I couldn't tell him it was because of me that she lost her job.

'Oh shit! That's not good. The day we break up, she loses her job,' Tejas said.

'Suspended for the rest of the year. Farah is calling it health leave in her mail to everyone. You really broke up?'

'I didn't plan it. I just wanted Farah to assign you to my portfolio, to take a load off Aisha.'

'It's all too much for her. She hasn't been doing well.'

'I have never seen her this angry.'

'She's been slipping in office too – wardrobe malfunctions, food spilt on her clothes, hair a mess, the whole shebang. Her own site is getting nothing but hate comments,' I added.

'How was she after I left?'

'Don't ask. She kept bingeing on my Hershey's Kisses and walked to the smoking area every fifteen minutes. I'm sure she smelt awful by the time she went for her appraisal.'

'Still, if anyone can recover from this, it's Aisha.'

'I hope so. Shall we get started then?'

'Started on what? You want to eat something?'

'Focus, Tejas. Your social media. Aisha has posts scheduled for everyone for the remainder of the year, except you. I have to figure out yours. The rest of my time is going to go for JLF.'

'Wow. Way to go! Finally. That's great, Ruhi. Now all you have to do is work your ass off.'

'There's no need to be sarcastic. Some of us actually like our jobs.'

'Fine, fine, just kidding. You know what, I give you free rein. I have enough going on with my novel and can't do this with you. Why don't you just do that on your own? It's what Aisha would do. The site and page are for my fans. You are my number one fan. What do you want to know?'

'Hm, I could do a post about this cafe. Your favourite places in Delhi, restaurants, cafes, bars. Then we could move on to movies, music.'

'There you go. Problem solved. I'll always be available to even go to these places with you. For pictures and so on. I knew I made the right choice by choosing you.'

I was positively glowing.

'You're looking good, Ruhi.'

That caught me off guard. I wouldn't fall for it this time, though. Not immediately.

'It would be nice to go out together sometime. Professionally, or otherwise.'

I ignored that.

'How's your book going, Tejas? Another bestseller in the making?'

'All right, can't complain.'

'We need it next to next Monday. Whatever you have.'

'Seriously? I thought the deadline was December.'

'Don't look so morose. You have a couple of weeks to spruce up whatever you're working on.'

'Morose doesn't begin to describe it.'

19

Hot, Cold & Hot Again

– TEJAS –

Saturday, 28 October

What an idea, to drop everything in life and to just focus on that one thing. What a scary thought not to have a plan B. Delusion feeds success. What about being safe? I do understand, having a safety net is important. But it's not a risk. And sometimes the only things worth doing are the scariest things. But the land beyond is magical. Well, seems magical. Just like this did. There is no magic to happen. It is all about doing it, creating things by one's own self. Maybe doing something slightly crazy might be in order. Maybe giving up how I feel, is in order. Maybe just doing things is in order. What else, being brave, being audacious. Grabbing things. Nicely. Being a smart mouth. Being awkward. Being. Getting inspired. Allowing myself to be inspired. By people. Places. Objects. Music. Scenarios.

It's been two weeks since Aisha and I split, and I cannot pen down a word. It hurts like somebody put a stake through my body.

Stop thinking about Aisha, I told myself. *Focus, man. Focus.* Postponing the book isn't going to work much longer. I had to push out something. Then again, genius took time.

I made a drink. Maybe I'd have a Coleridge-type epiphany if I passed out. I sat with my drink in one hand and cigarette in the other.

I just couldn't get a decently balanced sentence out. I finished my whiskey, downed two more and began reading my notes.

The church was built on the skeletons of those who'd died. It was a tourist attraction, picturesque with its Gothic towers and ravens flying appropriately for tourists to click pictures good enough to be on postcards.

Little did they know the bloodstained history of the walls and windows that they clicked with their oversized cameras.

Eons ago, a man lived there, seemingly alone. He wanted for nothing. He had all one could ask for. The man had a secret. In his dungeons were two young girls, tied and kept. Before the depths of the man's depravity were explored, it was clear, he had chains around his ankles too and the key was with the lady in power.

I woke up sweating. What kind of a twisted dream was that? I couldn't bear to remember it, forget use it. Was I being held against my will by Farah, and in that exact manner, kept Aisha and Ruhi as playthings?

I wasn't doing that.

I needed time and this situation would have to fix itself. It will have to bide its time out like a hangover.

I had to get out of the house and there was only one place I could think of going to at this hour. And it was her birthday.

~⁓~

My life was in shambles, it was even all over social media, but Aisha saw our breakup as an opportunity to celebrate.

The driveway was full of cars – I spotted the latest Mercedes and Beamer. I had a set of Aisha's garage keys in my car and had no trouble parking. Hip-hop music thudded out of the house and people I'd never seen before were spilling onto the house lawns.

I spotted Aisha in a shimmery black dress.

'Hello, boyfriend,' she said spotting me, champagne bottle in hand. 'Meet all my best friends.'

'These are not your friends. I can't spot Ruhi,' I said.

'That's because backstabbers weren't invited,' Aisha said. 'Excuse me. Kaaartikk?' she stumbled over to a fair, perpetually annoyed-looking fellow.

'I need you,' I texted Ruhi. 'Can you come to Aisha's place? Emergency.'

'On my way!' she texted back.

I didn't want to make a fool of myself; this party already had enough of them, with Aisha obliviously following around her infamous ex and the giggling gaggle of girls who kept pointing at me but did not come by to talk. Some party.

There was no one I was remotely interested in having a conversation with until Ruhi arrived, looking splendid in a red dress flanked by Ani and Rahul, one of Litracy's in-house designers.

'I didn't know you guys were that close by,' I told Ruhi.

'What's the emergency?'

'Are you still fighting with Aisha?' I said into her ear, over the music.

'I haven't seen her after she got fired. Why'd you need me?' she hollered back. 'What was so urgent? Isn't it her birthday today?'

'I have to talk to you. Let's go inside.'

'Hang on.' Ruhi grabbed a wine bottle and two glasses.

'I don't think Aisha should see me though.'

We took to an inconspicuous corner of the living room. She poured me a glass.

'Is it me or does Aisha look slimmer than before? I had no idea she had this many friends,' Ruhi said.

'She doesn't. They're just people she knows.'

'So is it about the deadline?' Ruhi said.

'What?'

'Did you call me to talk to Farah about your deadline?'

'Yes and no. It would be great if you can.'

'I figured, with your breakup.'

'That's actually what I wanted to talk to you about. I don't have Aisha anymore and I thought we really connected again.'

'Are you high, Tejas?'

'I'm serious, that's what I am. I haven't been doing okay after the breakup. I feel like I hurt her and you. It's tormenting me, Ruhi.'

'You are so dramatic.'

'And you sound exactly like Aisha.'

'No, I mean, channel this, access this in your writing. Write what you feel, Tejas. Get it all out. Have you written about this?'

'No.' I'd been numbing it for days.

'You are not going to be able to write happy stuff. Don't worry about Farah, I'll handle her.'

'*You'll* handle her?'

Aisha's room door flung open. A flustered Aisha walked out. She tripped, took off her heels and threw them back at someone in her bedroom.

'You disgust me. Get out of my house, you shallow prick,' she shouted.

'Fuck, Aisha. It's not my fault you've become a pig.' Kartik emerged, buttoning his shirt.

'You and your sister are nothing but snobs.'

'At least we aren't fat,' he said.

Ruhi's jaw dropped. 'You need to talk to Aisha. I'll mingle. I'm sure she doesn't want to see me. You're a little tipsy, but you'll manage.'

Aisha was in the kitchen, trying to find a glass, presumably.

'Here.' I put some water in a glass and led her to the sofa. She promptly finished it and poured the wine in the glass.

'This is a nightmare. Do you ever think your life is a nightmare, Tejas?'

'All the time,' I said.

'You should have seen Kartik's face, Tejas. Like, he never protested when I was a bag of bones, that stuck-up fuck. If I see him again, I'm going to punch him. I threw this party all because of him. What a stupid thing for me to do. I should have been happy with you. Do you think us splitting up was a mistake?' she said.

'No. I miss you but I can't handle two people's problems together.'

'Which two people?' she asked, counting on her fingers, slurring the words.

'You and me,' I told her. Then she fell asleep on the sofa.

I found Ruhi talking to a group of people who were absorbed in a story she was telling. It seemed to be about a tantrum a particular author threw every time she went to Litracy. I waited till she finished.

'How are you getting home?' I asked Ruhi.

'I have a car and driver.'

'I really need to talk to you. More wine?'

'Okay.' She giggled.

'What's so funny?'

'What a mess I made of us.'

'It's my fault too.'

'I know it sounds awful, but I'm a little glad things didn't end well with you and Aisha.'

'I'm finding it atrociously hard to be on my own. I can't write, I can't sleep, I can't do anything productive. I need your energy back in my life. You completely stopped talking to me after we got back.'

'You didn't bother being honest with me and when Aisha caught your eye, you dumped me like trash. I *saw* you guys in the plane.'

'It wasn't like that, Ruhi.'

'Holding hands. What you and Aisha did hurt me. You know, I had your journal all along. I tore up each page and threw it away.'

'I had a feeling.' I took her hand. 'I need you, Ruhi.'

'I've changed. I don't think I'm a good person anymore, Tejas.' She took a cigarette and lit it flawlessly. She took a deep inhale and looked away from my face to her shoes.

'When Aisha took my position in the JLF team—'

'It wasn't yours.'

'It was mine. *Is* mine now. I know the festival in and out and I deserved it. It was clearly too much for Aisha to handle. Anyway, I was so mad, Tejas. She took you, she took my position at work, my hardworking reputation was overshadowed by her flamboyance – so I had her fired.'

'You had her fired?'

'I didn't mean to. I just clicked a picture of you guys fighting and showed it to Ani. Before I knew it, it was online. We wrote a scathing story that made her look bad during appraisals. I just wanted to circulate it within WD and definitely not online. I just wanted a little revenge. I hate myself, Tejas. I thought she would get kicked off the core festival team for having her emotions all over the place, not actually lose her job. I could have stopped Ani.'

'I'm not going to deny that Aisha partially helped dig the pit she's in right now, with her mood swings and mismanagement of time, but it's Farah you should have stood up to. Aisha did not pick the JLF team. Your mother did. As for me, I did the right thing, maybe at the wrong time. Nothing earth-shattering.'

'I feel worse.'

'Aisha should be dealing with her health anyway.'

'But her job, she lost her job.'

'Suspended. It's not totally your fault. And it's not as if she's on the road; her family is supporting her, and she's busy partying. There are other ways to earn and she's a bit of a celebrity. She'll be fine.'

'Really?'

'Yes. I think it's great you fought for what you wanted.'

'What is this, then? Are we dating again?' Ruhi asked me.

'I'd like that. I want you to think about it and not rush into it though.'

'You've been hot and cold and tepid, it's too much drama for me. I'm not Aisha.'

'Which is why I choose you. I need someone stable, and it's you.'

'Oh, Tejas,' she said. 'I should leave, it's past two. First, I want to check on Aisha.'

The house was empty. The last of the people had left and the music had stopped.

I picked up Aisha from the sofa and put her on her bed and put the speaker and bottles of alcohol in the house.

Ruhi put a glass of water on Aisha's bedside table but she wouldn't let me wake her up in front of her.

After she left, I shook Aisha awake and told her I was locking the house and leaving.

'Bye, boyfriend,' she said.

'I'm not your boyfriend anymore.'

20

All Time Low

– AISHA –

Sunday, 29 October

What's on your mind?

Dear fans! Your fave blogger just completed a super stint with Litracy Books. Another feather in her cap in time to turn twenty-six! Stay tuned to @EveryDelhiGirl for a flashback in publishing, coming soon!

Mortified.

There is no other way to describe how I felt after the humiliation of last night. Kartik snubbed me in front of Tejas and then I passed out in front of him. That was the third time he'd seen me unconscious. I could sink no lower. And he'd taken care of me yet again. That was worse. I wonder if he felt guilty for initiating the chain of events that led to me being fired.

Nevertheless, there was no room for him in my life, though I had room for a lot of things now.

In the two weeks since I'd stopped going to work, I had started working out, hired a maid to cook healthy home food, thrown a party and doubled my efforts to bring traffic to my blog.

I couldn't helped checking out Tejas's blog and Facebook. His Facebook page was blowing up. It featured Tejas's favourite cafe and bar. Ruhi had taken my blogging method and used them for his posts. Good for *her*.

I felt like the main character in a movie who was at her lowest and had to learn to pick herself up. I'd just skip the sad part and go to the picking-myself-up part. I didn't need the tears.

I still had myself and my blog, granted my self was bigger than I ever could imagine, but I was doing everything I could with what I had.

That was how I found myself in the gym on a Sunday morning, despite having the worst hangover of my life.

I was in a white t-shirt and black track pants with bright pink shoes. I felt flabby and paunchy at my fifty-nine kilos. Everyone around me was crazy fit. There were girls in sports bras and guys in muscle shirts. No one so much as glanced at me.

Losers.

Some months ago, I could have given those girls a run for their money with my outfits and body and attitude. I actually never thought I'd be here, I used to make fun of people sweating and working hard, just so they could look good naked.

At this gym, there were people around who all knew each other and I felt invisible, like someone had transplanted someone else's mind inside my body. Still, I was a fighter. I'd lost six kilos in two weeks and simply had to work harder.

I finished the treadmill and abs, then began the weights. I was beginning to feel dizzy but I'd get through it. I hadn't eaten this morning, I couldn't stomach the thought of food, and all the better for it. I would push myself harder and the fat would burn off.

I was doing burpees on the stepper. Before I knew it, I had blacked out.

When I came to, I was on the floor, there were people around me, my left sneaker was lying on the side next to the dumbbell and a gym trainer was pressing a towel full of ice to my foot.

'Relax, ma'am, you fell on your leg. A doctor was in the spa, she's coming to look at you.'

And sure enough a young lady in a bathrobe came to look at my leg. Soon there was a puddle around us, and I learnt that I'd fainted (again) while exercising and fallen on my leg. She removed the ice. My foot had swollen to double its size. Thank God I couldn't feel anything. I felt even sicker. Someone gave me lemonade in a disposable glass.

'Aisha, right?' she said.

'How long will your parents take to get here?'

'They're not around.'

'Do you have anyone you can call? Someone, a friend or a boyfriend. This needs to be looked at immediately.'

That made me smile. This lady thought I was attractive enough to have a boyfriend.

'Is it a sprain? I'll take a cab home. Can I do that?' I looked at the trainers who were still standing around, looking worried.

'I can come with you to the hospital if you like. We'll tell them to administer local anaesthesia, first thing.'

'It isn't a sprain?' I moved my toe, and a sharp pain spread up my leg. 'OW. No. It's broken,' I cried out.

'Ice,' she told the trainer, who moved back into position. 'Don't move your leg at all. I'm calling an ambulance.'

'Ambulance?'

'Do you want me to inform someone? They can meet you at the hospital and take you home.'

I gave her my phone and told her who to call.

When the ambulance arrived, I assured the doctor I'd be okay and she didn't need to come. She gave me her number and told me to call her if I needed anything.

'You tell them you're a friend of mine, they'll do everything quickly.'

~⁀

'Thank you,' I told Ruhi.

'Ya it's like deja vu.'

I was in the backseat of her car, my left leg stretched out in the cast. She was quiet; I had to make most of the conversation. She paid the hospital bill too without a word, as I didn't have my wallet with me.

'You've started driving, that's cool,' I told her.

'Yes.'

'You look really good. The contact lenses suit you,' I told her.

'Thanks. I would have thought you would be at home, getting over the entire office thing.'

'I'm not the kind to sit around and mope, you know that. You can park anywhere,' I told Ruhi when we pulled into the driveway. 'The closer the better as you'll have to help me in.'

Ruhi just sat looking ahead with her hands on the steering wheel.

'Why didn't you tell Farah I was dating Tejas too?' she said. 'You had pictures of us. From Bhutan. In your phone.'

'I don't know why,' I said. 'You've worked hard. You deserved the position. Plus it wasn't your boss, it was your mother I'd be tattling to.'

She was silent. We entered and Ruhi sat me down on a sofa.

'So how does it feel? To have won?' I blurted out without thinking.

She sighed.

'You have everything you ever wanted. It's not enough, is it?' I asked.

'I wouldn't have done what you did to me,' she said.

'*I* would never have done anything to put your job in jeopardy,' I said. 'I just took what was offered to me. Tejas hit on me after you'd broken up. I never ever brought you down in public. The second somebody else waltzed in and threatened you, you're getting ready to turn around and run. You can't define yourself with other people. You can only define yourself. Look at you, look at how good it is to see a bit of personality coming out of you.'

'You do know I took the picture that had you suspended.'

'I guessed. I'm not petty, Ruhi. I wasn't going to spearhead an investigation, I was already out of office. If I did tell Farah, it would have made things worse for you. Plus, don't tell me she wasn't happy with the publicity Tejas got for free? And I'm sure you weren't working alone in the first place. You don't have the heart for it, Ruhi.'

'I'm so sorry, Aisha. I got carried away with Ani.'

'Why don't you make some tea? Let's talk about something else.'

Ruhi fixed us two cups of green tea. The highlights in her hair caught my eye. Mine had gone out.

'It's so good to see you,' Ruhi told me, setting my cup next to me and sitting down. 'Did you know, I always wanted a cast in school, so all my friends could write on it with sketch pens?'

'You can be the first to write on mine.'

'There's another thing you should know. I crashed your party last night along with Ani and Rahul.'

'What? You got her to my house? And really, Rahul?'

'Tejas called me. We were in GK,' Ruhi said.

'Oh no. Did you see—' I began saying.

'Kartik is a dick.'

'I'm so embarrassed. Did you put me to bed?' I asked.

'Tejas and I did, yes.'

'Thanks, Ruhi.'

'The least I could do,' she said.

'How's Tejas doing?'

'Uh – actually there's one more thing you should know.'

'It's okay if you guys are having a thing again.' I rolled my eyes.

'He said he needed me. And I know I'm ready.'

'I'm sure you are. You're like a new person. Can I give you a little advice though?' I asked.

'You won't take no for an answer.'

'Ruhi, what will help you is to date – date as many people as you want. You need to learn to say no and take a no. You need to deal with the biggest problem in your life which is—'

'I know – Farah. Tejas told me.'

'Tejas is dumb. The problem is, you need to stop wanting to be liked by everyone.'

'I want to be like you, everyone loves you.'

'No, everyone respects me, including Farah. Few people like me.'

'No!'

'Yes! You're already getting there. Look at the position I'm in because of you.'

'I'm so sorry again.'

'This wasn't even in Farah's hands. It wasn't even the call of the round-spectacled HR lady.'

'Then?'

'I know how important looks and impressions are at work. I let things slide. No one is to blame but me. I got distracted, let my health go downhill and ignored Tejas. I would have done the same if I had an employee like that.'

'Are you visiting your dietician?'

'We Skyped last week. She's on vacation.' I hadn't seen her for months but I didn't want to have that conversation with Ruhi.

'Do you want to know about Tejas now?'

'Oh yes.'

'He really misses you.'

'What else is new?'

'He's too heartbroken to work.'

'But not heartbroken enough to date you? Ruhi, I told Farah this and I'm telling you too. He is in a rut which he needs to come out of. If you try to do his work, along with the festival tasks, your own editorial job and mine, you'll snap. He is so far gone, he'll get you in trouble. His entire book is overdue for you guys. I know he doesn't have a word written.'

'He says he'll work it out. I spoke to him, I believe—'

'He says a lot of things. Don't make my mistake. Tejas doesn't have to know if you tell Farah.'

'Hmm.'

'And you know how Tejas led you on before. If my instinct tells me anything, it's that you shouldn't let him get too close. I'm not saying that because I want him back or anything. Just be cautious okay? He's dealing with a lot too.'

Ruhi was quiet and twirled her biscuit around on the table instead of eating it.

'Trust yourself. Not Tejas, not me.'

'And are you going to look for work, or...'

'I'm going to give my blog a makeover, focus all my attention on it. Once I get my groove back, I'll apply to places.'

'Any chance of coming back to Litracy?'

'No way.'

'Well, if you need any contacts and if you need company in the coming weeks, let me know.'

'Please. You're going to drown in office work.'

'I'll try anyway.'

⌒∾

Tuesday, 25 October

What's on your mind?

@EveryDelhiGirl counts down the best girl-centric sitcoms of the year. Tune in to see if your fave show made the list! #netflixandchill

I have been binge-watching every show about fat young girls I could find. There are hardly any. They're always the main character's sidekick. And Ugly Betty? I hated her. Why can't the protagonists of these shows be chubby and sassy? It's always chubby and sweet. That's not me. I don't exist.

I used to be a star, now I'm a black hole that swallows up everything edible that comes before it. Has that part of me died forever?

I tried to ignore these thoughts that began occupying my head. All I had for company was my laptop. I had no friends I could call to come over except Ruhi, and it was a weekday.

I'd written out a plan to revamp my blog and I forced myself to check the traffic every day though it was getting lower and lower, from triple to double digits.

It wasn't as if I could keep posting pictures of my cast. Even the stray cat I'd taken a snap or two of, and took to feeding leftovers got more likes than I did.

I'd started creating posts out of whatever selfies I had, which included horribly overweight pictures from my last weeks at work. However, I had to work with what I'd got.

When I logged on, I saw a comment! Finally, after days. I'd be happy to see even a negative comment.

One guy had posted: Congratulations!

That sounded promising. Did he like my post 'Sassy Yet Sensible Work Wear'? If the commenter was a man, why would he congratulate me on women's wear?

'Thank you!'

He replied immediately. 'When are you due?'

WHAT? Was this guy serious?

Dear Manhole,
Just because a girl has a healthy-looking body does not mean she is pregnant. Please get that inside your head. You are the reason girls around the world starve themselves to death.

Please fuck off the internet and don't visit this site, ever ever again.

Best,
Aisha.

I hobbled over to the window, cracked it open and lit a cigarette. This was outrageous. The kind of freaks I had to deal with. I calmed myself before I went online and wrote even worse things.

When I went back, I tried to view the comments, but I couldn't open my site's dashboard. I tried for about half an hour and then checked my mail. I found an email from my blogging platform saying my site had been pulled down due to the hate comment posted by me. ME. How? I was defending myself against verbal abuse.

I flung my laptop off the bed and threw my coffee cup at the wall. It broke, the black coffee staining the wall like blood.

'*Kya hua, help chahiye*?' My maid entered.

'Leave me alone!' I yelled.

I felt like shoving the dented laptop out into the garden and setting it aflame.

Maybe there was something to it. Maybe I was happier being the skinny bitch since every damn person liked her more. Maybe there was something to being size zero and talking only about fashion and clothes and style.

Six months ago, I had EVERYTHING. And now?

I was done.

21

(You Drive Me) Crazy

– RUHI –

Friday, 20 November

To Do:
- *JLF blog*
- *Press kit*
- *Follow-up with authors*
- *Brainstorm panel discussions*
- *Go to salon, waxing, blow-dry*

This was going to be the scariest thing I'd ever done.

I was sitting across the table from Tejas, looking at the meal he had cooked for me in his giant dining room. Two glasses of wine sat on the table. After meeting Aisha, I took the leap. It wasn't a bed of roses but there had been many flowers along the way. It was going to be *the* night, and this time I didn't have a sliver of doubt. We'd been dating for a month, no hidden agendas.

Ironically, since Tejas and Aisha began dating, and that moment on the flight, I'd been feeling alive. Yes, a lot of hate was there and I couldn't look Aisha in the face for weeks, but at least I wasn't hiding behind some glossy veneer, faking my emotions. I'd slowly but surely discarded my old self, which, as Aisha had pointed out, had been holding me back.

Tejas poured me my second glass of wine.

'I thought she'd call me,' Tejas said. 'I live closer.'

'Me too.' I was telling him how Aisha broke her leg.

'She must be really mad at me.'

'Actually, you're the last thing on her mind. She's planning out her whole life, social media, healthy eating, next year, sitting in one place. Ambitious, no doubt, but I don't think she'll lose any more weight like that.'

'Oh. And her parents?'

'They won't be coming back this year.'

'How's she gonna manage?'

'Crutches and stuff. She has help to cook and clean.'

'And you spoke to her, finally, about everything? She wasn't mad at you about us being together?'

I took his hand. 'She's the last person you need to worry about. How are you doing?'

'I've been thinking,' Tejas said.

'You need more time for the book?' I asked.

'No, well – yes – but I've actually been thinking about us.'

'You know, I've changed, it's different now. I can feel it, can't you?' I said.

'I need support at the moment, Ruhi.'

'I'm here for that. I know I'm working too much and my mother is being a b—'

'I'm not in a good place, I'm still suffering through the breakup.'

I left his hand and stood up.

'I don't want to hurt you again,' he said.

'You're in a fucking relationship, Tejas. Not a breakup. You hit on *me*, starting the day you broke up with Aisha. "*Are you dating anyone, Ruhi? It would be nice to go out together sometime, Ruhi. I need you, Ruhi.*" Who do you think you are? The heartbreaker of the world? You can't touch me, Tejas.'

'I really fell for Aisha. It's been hard. You're a good person and I'm asking you.'

'Asking me for what? You don't know what you want. Tell me now.'

'I like being around you, but not in that way.'

'Fair enough. No more drama.' I picked up my bag and began putting on my heels.

'Where are you going? Aren't we friends?' Tejas said.

'How could you even ask me that? All these months, throughout the year, you've been stringing me along,' I said. 'So please excuse me, if I don't want to be friends with you.'

'You're rejecting me as a friend?'

'Yes, Tejas, I am. Let's keep it professional,' I told him. 'No more extensions, no more excuses. I'm not taking the fall for you anymore.'

'I never asked you to.'

'God, Tejas, Aisha was right. You are so deep in your own little rabbit hole of shit, you don't want to come out of it and take responsibility.'

'I can't turn it on and off, Ruhi. You know that's not how writers work. This is happening because you met Aisha and she filled your head with all this. You've seen me through my book.'

'And I've also seen how I've had to take your half-baked writing and turn it into a real book.'

'You don't write for me, Ruhi. You edit. Who are you to write for me?'

'Are you homesick for hell?' I was yelling now. 'If I had stopped all the support and suggestions I gave you back in February before you signed the contract—'

'I would have done it anyway without you. Maybe a few weeks later, maybe a few weeks earlier, and a better job of it, too. You bled my time dry and in addition to that, dragged me to the office every other week for pointless meetings. I am treated like an employee, not a writer.'

'That is absolutely not true,' I said. 'You don't trust your own art. You don't know what the hell is going on inside your head and this is what you do, manipulate and twist till we become minions who do your bidding. You're too scared to own up to your own life.'

'Who are you, Ruhi? You're turning into a bigger bitch than Aisha.'

'Aisha was honest and you couldn't deal with her either. She's in a fucked-up state because of you, Tejas.'

'No, she got fired because of you.'

'I didn't go to Farah behind her back in the office.'

'Well I didn't Snapchat and Instagram our pictures all over Delhi.'

'Good job. You're such a hero. You also didn't date me to break up with me one more time.'

'I was protecting you, Ruhi.'

'I'm not a child! You say I have to stand up for myself and then you treat me like this? You know what, Aisha has moved on. I will get over you too. But you will never get over yourself.'

⌒⌒

'So you decided to return home after all,' I heard my mother's voice in the dark.

'Mom. You scared me! I wasn't expecting you back tonight.'

'Clearly. It's midnight, young lady, do you have any idea how many missed calls I've given you, how worried I've been?'

'Don't start. Not right now,' I told her loudly. 'I know you're mad. Just shout at me tomorrow.' And I went to my room.

'Ruhi. Ruhi.' She stood at the door to my room.

'Please. Go away.'

I took out the box of keepsakes of my relationship with Tejas and smashed it on the floor.

'I hate you!' I screamed and cried till I fell asleep when my mother woke me with a cup of tea.

'I'm guessing that wasn't you yelling at me,' she said, looking at the things on the floor.

'Want to tell me what happened?'

'Okay.' And so I did.

22

Ghosts of Writings Past

– TEJAS –

Friday, 29 November

It comes. From things around me. It just randomly inserts itself into my head. Affecting and colouring my life for the next few hours. It's like a really bad trip. You know it. There's no clear way to get rid of it. It injects its poison into me. You try distracting yourself. It's overpowering. You can't even vent it all out in one go. You have to let it run its course. It's terrible. It gives you nightmares. In real life.

I was at my favourite bar in Delhi, PCO. I was meeting a lovely lady through Tindr. She was here and she looked quite all right.

This was my big plan to get my writing going again. It worked before, when I would write what was happening to me. I just had to have interesting things happen to me.

She worked in a bank, she said.

'Oh.' I didn't know what to say next.

She offered me the name of the bank.

'What is a successful banker like you doing on Tindr?' I asked.

'You know, what you're doing,' she said.

When we were at home, she mentioned she was getting married in a week, and this was her last act of rebellion. This freaked me out. I could write about it, sure. But it wasn't what I needed. I asked her to leave and spent a sleepless night tossing and turning. I couldn't bear to be alone in my bedroom.

This was my third conquest in seven days. I would just have to try again tomorrow.

I had a text from Aisha asking me to call her ASAP and one from Ruhi asking me to check my mail. Maybe Aisha wanted to get together and Ruhi's email would be a letter pleading with me to take her back.

I hadn't checked my mail in a while. I had a bunch of spam and five emails in my inbox. The first was from Farah with the subject: *Writing!* The second was another from her reinstating Ruhi as my social media manager and informing me that Aisha was no longer with the company. The third was a forwarded email to the entire publishing house stating that illicit relationships were strictly frowned upon. The remaining two emails both had the subject: *Imp. regd Tejas Sahni.* I sat up. One was from Ruhi to Farah which I was marked on and one from Farah to me.

This is an email regarding the behaviour of the author, Tejas Sahni. I have been working with him for eleven months now.

In addition to his lack of initiative to promote himself and adhere to his two-book contract, considering we launched him in good faith, he has been behaving unprofessionally on a consistent basis.

His attitude towards his work-in-progress has been completely lazy and he is becoming uncouth in his interactions with me.

He has not responded to emails from me or Farah regarding the book's status.

When spoken to in person, he is rude and unforthcoming about the book.

I have never worked with an author so egotistic. I refuse to work on any project related to him and urge that he be relieved of his contract so I can work with better authors with better sensibilities.

Oh god. Shit. What had she done? I couldn't believe my eyes. What the fuck had Ruhi done?

The email from Farah's personal account was timed at 1 a.m., the night Ruhi had come over.

Tejas,
I just had a chat with Ruhi. She told me what transpired between the two of you all year long and I am sorry I ever signed you on.

We are not interested in pursuing a second book with you. The royalties and print run of Carnival of Dreams stand as before.

You will get a revised contract by the end of the week.

Regards,
Farah

All this ... because of Aisha. Ruhi was not like this a year ago. Aisha had created a monster. Had she been sitting and planning this at home with Ruhi? Did she really even break her leg or was that all a fucking story?

I finished half the bottle of Jack Daniel's and went into the bedroom and sat and looked at the character sketches and notes, what I had been unable to build into anything for a book. I saw pages and pages of work left incomplete, like ghosts of writing past. I saw copies of my book. I hated it. I fucking hated it for putting me in this position. I was done. This was quits.

I locked the room. I poured whiskey from the bottle over the books and papers. My life was ruined because of them. I lit it and watched it burn.

Burn. Burn. Burn.

Burning my life away.

The flames crackled and hissed. There was smoke.

I saw the glint of paper, 'torrents of wastepaper baskets and sounds of heels'. That was the publishing house's description.

My work, all the little things I had been collecting and writing. I could just let it go and walk away from all this forever. The room was black with smoke. I knew I would pass out if I didn't do anything.

I took a blanket and managed to stop the flames. No staff woke up, thankfully.

I opened a window and switched on the fan. The carpet's corner had burned too. Well, I didn't care about that.

I sat outside and smoked a joint. I sat and watched the smoke of the fire that I built leave from the window.

~~~

Last night was unbelievable.

It was 6 a.m. The alcohol was gone.

I began to clean. Not a shred of the book I wrote remained.

There was a hole, a black hole in my desk. I began to laugh.

I sat at my desk and it just happened. I picked up a pen and I wrote. I wrote for six hours straight. I filled three notebooks. I wrote about the past few months, I wrote about Aisha and Ruhi. I wrote about myself.

I didn't stop to eat, drink, nothing. It just poured out. It all just poured out. There was so much I had to say. These weren't stories, but they were the stories I had been building up in my head. More real than the ones on paper, but God it felt so good just to get it all down.

I functioned better from being Tejas than being Tejas the writer.

I wondered if I would pick up the pen tomorrow. I decided I was going to. Even if it was shit.

When I stepped outside the house for some air, I saw a magazine posted under my door. It was an anthology of short stories and my submission was in print. I'd never sent it – it must have been Ruhi. Looking at my story in those pages I knew what my next book was going to be. All my writing over the past many days was pointing towards exactly that.

My next stop was at Litracy to see Ruhi and show her the magazine.

It was office lunchtime and when I got out of my car, who did I see but Ruhi with Rahul trailing along behind her. He lit what looked like a joint and passed it to Ruhi.

'I come in peace,' I said, startling her. She gave the joint back to the guy.

'It's a cigarette,' she said.

'Of course it is.'

'I'm not talking to you. I'll call security,' Ruhi said, turning away from me.

'Ruhi, Litracy doesn't have security. Don't freak out, I'm not angry.'

'I thought you'd want to kill me with your bare hands.'

'I'm not evil.'

She scowled.

'I came here to show you this.' She wasn't even looking at me. 'You were right, Ruhi. I was stuck.'

'You didn't have to come all the way here to tell me that.'

'Look.' I shoved the magazine under her nose. 'Tell me this doesn't make you happy.'

'No, it doesn't.'

'You sent it.'

'Tejas. If you have something to say, say it.' She glanced at Rahul.

'I don't blame you for what you did. In fact, I came to apologise. I was in a block. And now I'm out. And this,' I waved the magazine in front of her, 'has given me the idea for my next book.'

'Okay. We done?'

'I just wanted to thank you.'

'After everything, I don't have time for you. And I didn't send your work to that place,' Ruhi said, now flanked by Rahul. He put his arm around her, and they disappeared up into the Litracy building.

Of course, it was Aisha. Aisha showed me the light, when I didn't want to see it. Now it was my turn.

23

Monster in the Mirror

– AISHA –

Sunday, 30 November

Forty-nine kilos. The number shone at me from the weighing scale, which I'd somehow managed to balance on with my cast. It had to be a record of some kind, to lose ten kilos in six weeks.

I limped to the mantelpiece, tossed the empty food delivery boxes to the ground and lit a candle. I'd started feeding a stray cat that visited my garden. I opened the door and the cat attacked the leftovers. He was getting fatter and I was getting thinner.

Unlike the procession of diyas and rangoli that the help put up for Diwali parties, it was going to be a lonely one for me.

I'd planned out a lush evening for myself. I'd ordered in Chinese and a bottle of white wine was chilling in the fridge. I'd lined up *The Vampire Diaries, Gossip Girl* and *Gilmore Girls* on my computer and had the latest issues of *Vogue, Cosmo* and *Elle* waiting for me patiently. I was beginning to look like the girls on the shows and in the magazines, and some of my old clothes were fitting me too!

I was hungry most of the time, but I'd found a way to eat and not put on weight. I was on a steady diet of coffee, cigarettes and one meal a day.

I'd just settled in on my bed when the doorbell rang. I decided to ignore it. I wasn't in a state to be seen and the house was a mess. My parents's friends knew they were away and there was no one I was expecting. Ruhi was supposed to drop by but had too much work and so had cancelled last minute. Work was driving her mad, she'd said.

I heard a noise. Maybe the cat was going through the garbage again, he was already jittery because of the crackers.

'Hey there pussycat,' I heard a voice say.

'Tejas, is that you?' I called out. He had a key.

'The one and only.'

'Hang on a sec.' I looked for a gown, a shawl, something to cover up over the tank top and shorts I was wearing and threw the blanket over myself. 'Come in now.'

'Hiding something?' he said, leaning on the doorframe.

'No, just old clothes. You, wow. You're here.'

'Yes. Are you still upset?'

He enveloped me in a tight wrap. He smelled and looked so much better than I could remember.

'You look…'

'Fractured?'

'Ill. Are you okay? Do you want me to call someone?' he said, touching my forehead. 'You're a bit warm. And thin.'

'I'm fine. Just strong painkillers.'

'Still?' He gave me a goofy smile. 'And the mess in the kitchen? You had a party again, didn't you?'

I hadn't met anyone since I broke my leg and the mess was all me, but of course I didn't tell him that.

'Why are you here?'

'It's Diwali.'

'You're not angry with me anymore?'

'Look.' He showed me the anthology of young Indian writers.

'They published you? Oh my God!'

'Yes. All thanks to you. Let's sit and talk. Should I make coffee?'

'I have wine here.'

'It's four in the afternoon.'

'We have something to toast.'

'Okay, I'll dig up glasses.'

'Hang on, I got some right here.' I put my hand under the bed and pulled out a couple of water glasses. I wiped the dust off of them with a tissue.

'What are we toasting to? The story?' I asked.

'My second book.'

'Really? It's done?'

'No it's begun. And my writer's block has vanished.'

'Are you sure?'

'One draft. Stop second-guessing me.'

'Okay, fine, fine.' I was too tired to argue. He took my hand.

'Thank you, Aisha.'

'I would have done it all over again to see this day,' I said.

'I'm grateful,' Tejas said. 'And glad to see you. Though you've lost a hell lot of weight. I mean I thought you would be—'

'Fatter?'

'Healthier.'

'Cigarette?' I asked, fishing for an ashtray under my bed.

'Here?'

'Just open that window.'

'The room will smell of cracker smoke.'

'It already does. I don't mind.'

'Do you have a decent diet, Aisha? What about your dietician?'

'She's travelling.'

'Your maid cooks for you, right?'

'I fired the maid.'

'Why?'

'Don't ask. PMS.'

'What do you eat?'

'I tend to order in.'

'That's it. I'm going to stay here with you.'

'Tonight? Because...?'

'Because you need help. Till your cast comes off.'

'I can take care of myself. I always take care of myself. And it's just a few weeks away.'

'I need to be away from my house. There was a small fire. I need a break from that room.'

'Aren't there enough rooms in your mansion for you to hide in?'

'This will be perfect and so much fun.'

'I guess.'

'I'll go right now and bring my stuff.'

'Right now?' I asked.

'Right now. Don't worry about a thing.'

～〜⁓

Sunday, 7 December

Dear Diary,

I feel like an old woman. Tejas is treating me like one too. I've stopped asking him for anything but he's so enthusiastic. He insisted on taking me to and from the loo and this morning he helped me have a bath. It wasn't anything he hadn't seen before but I felt helpless. More so because of how he looks at me, with pity. I mean, it's just a broken leg.

Maybe he was feeling guilty for everything.

Today he made me get up and go to the kitchen too. He had cleaned the entire thing. Spotless.

Contrary to what I thought having him around would be like – watching movies all day, drinking wine and smoking – he spends all day writing and cooking and makes me eat two big meals in front of him. He hardly smokes up or drinks anymore and gives me a look when I ask for a second glass of wine.

When he's not reading me drafts of his new book, he's reading me literature, seriously.

He keeps asking me what I'm going to do with my life and if any blogs have hired me yet. He's even been complaining that I should cut back on smoking as I was getting irritable. Yes I was, but anyone would be if they had a foot in a cast for days on end.

In other news, I can see my cheekbones, I'm losing inches rapidly and will be back to normal in no time. If I am to reach my goal of forty kilos, I'll have to stop all this food I've been eating. I cannot bloat up again and go back to that monster in the mirror.

There's only one way I can reach my size by the end of this month and that is to not digest it. I can do that. Tejas will never find out.

I feel deceptive but no one asked him to be here. I know it's not the right thing to do but I have no choice.

24

Sorry Not Sorry
– RUHI –

Thursday, 7 December

To Do:
- *Consolidate who is staying where for JLF + assign intern to this*
- *Media coverage con-call*
- *Art and installation tie-ins*
- *Restaurants & cafes in Jaipur to partner this year*
- *Meeting to finalise panel*
- *Check with designers & interns on Litracy's goings-on*

Life was a drug. You couldn't do it forever. You needed to cut back. Go to rehab every once in a while to keep sane. They called them holidays, retreats where we'd abuse alcohol, but our drug was always the real world.

The routine of working for something which does nobody any real good is what would get us high. Peer pressure and acceptance, the adoration from the eyes of others, not within, is what would keep us high.

Is that why so many people who got the adoration, wasted away with drugs? Is it drugs or is it that they spent their lives living from the outside rather than the inside…

'Holiday rejected huh?' Rahul said, sitting beside me, interrupting my thoughts. The half of the edit room which was mine was more cluttered than ever before. It looked like the desk of a government office.

'I applied for this six months ago,' I told him. 'My mother knows my cousin's tickets are booked.'

'Where are you going?'

'Singapore.'

'Food haven.'

'Is it? I'll never know.'

'Don't do that to yourself. You got a good enough reason to go for this. She didn't even give you Diwali off. You missed my party.' He gave me a playful punch on the shoulder. I was beginning to think he liked me. 'If I were you, I'd write back marking her boss. You didn't even get selected for the JLF team in the first place.'

'Thanks for reminding me.'

'Do this later. Let's grab a smoke.'

'No thanks.'

I was standoffish but I hoped he'd understand. I had a lot on my mind. I set up my Skype and got ready to sign in, a sinking feeling in my stomach.

Ever since I took a leap of faith and told my mother what happened between Tejas and I over the past few months, her demeanour changed. She went from being concerned about my workload and stress, to callous and judgemental overnight. Because my issues were 'guy-related', she deemed them non-existent.

The aftermath of Tejas's release from his contract within Litracy's walls was negligible. Except Farah seemed to have taken it personally, that I had disappointed her, that it made her look bad Tejas didn't meet his deadlines. She made it evident whenever she got the chance.

The meeting I was conferencing in was to finalise the last remaining panelists with room for changes and backups. I called Ani instead of Farah, so that she couldn't chat and nag me at the same time.

The CEO led the discussion and then passed it over to Farah.

'Ruhi can write the panelists's bios and come up with the topics for the brochure,' Farah told the room. 'There are about three hundred panels.'

'I'm working on the blogging competition for the delegates and also selecting and assigning all volunteers their tasks. This is something the five interns can finish in a few days.'

'I will decide what the interns are to do. You please do what you've been asked.'

I could barely keep my head straight for the rest of the meeting. I don't know how I got through the questions and answers Her Highness put me through, and I got home and smoked the joint Rahul had given me, to use alone in case of emergency.

I had the house to myself. I put on a little light music and lit a few candles. The joint was supposed to help me relax and sleep but I just fell into deep thought. Of why I'd joined the publishing house, why I'd picked science in eleventh and twelfth grade but done Mass Communication in college.

It was because I wanted to find books I loved and share them with the world. Maybe they would help young people who felt like misfits like they'd helped me in school.

Just because I was the editor of the college paper and loved books, didn't mean I was too dumb to do anything else. I'd joined this place because I wanted to handle projects and books from beginning to the end. I had a professional degree. I hadn't signed up to be an editor to hide behind my glasses and my desk.

As part of the JLF team, I could be leading the social media division or marketing or PR if I chose. I'd been denigrated to the tasks that were in an intern's job description.

Carnival of Dreams, the copy from my box, was lying next to the candle. That's how it all began with Tejas. Now it was over. It gave me goose bumps to think I'd done all that on my own.

Then I lost my bearings even though I was in my own house. I felt like I was falling. I made my way to my bed and lay down.

I was guilty. I felt like Farah's behaviour was retribution for my actions to have Aisha and Tejas kicked off Litracy.

Tejas's words echoed in my ears. Had I really turned out to be a bigger bitch than her? I didn't care where my mind took me. What was a 'bitch' anyway? A man in power who behaved like that would be called rude or curt at the most and people would back off. Whereas a woman in charge who employed professionalism over sweetness to keep peers and juniors in check would be subject to backbiting and judgement.

I had to do what I did, right?

Wrong. I was a horrid person. This was my dark, horrible side. I had to face it. If I was selfish and continued to be so, so be it. This was me. At least it was the most honest I've ever been.

I wobbled to the candle, took it and the book to my loo, locked the door, opened the exhaust and began tearing out the pages like I'd done once before. I was going to turn my pity party of a life into a real party. I lit the pages on fire in the middle of the floor, leaving the cover aside. I'd finally destroyed every belonging of Tejas's that had been with me.

I thought of my mother. I knew she had pressures of her own, but it felt like she was out to get me. It wasn't even her fault. There was no excuse for the way I'd let her treat me. I got out my Litracy contract and added it to the pyre.

I watched it till I was hypnotised, and felt drowsy and sweaty. I put the ash on a newspaper and flushed it. The floor was hot where I'd made my little bonfire.

I checked my mail, just for fun. Farah had emailed me again saying I absolutely couldn't take even a day off till New Year's. In fact, the holidays I'd taken for Bhutan would need to be made up for on Saturdays till JLF.

I hadn't expected any better. I replied, asking for a time tomorrow to speak with her.

~

Friday, 8 December

To Do:
• *no tasks today!*

Farah had given me the time of 3 p.m. but wasn't free till 5 p.m. I'd been at White Dog all day waiting for this. Rahul was on standby, sending me thumbs-up emoticons on WhatsApp.

'Farah, I had certain expectations when I joined Litracy and it's been tough for me,' I said, sitting down.

'Is this about your holiday?'

'It's about my leaving.' I wanted to say it was about how I was treated by her. Instead, I added, 'The whole Tejas thing has been too much for me. It's for my emotional well-being. I can't take any more stress from anyone at this point.'

'Ruhi, you can't just walk out while in the middle of such a big project.'

'I can present you with a psych. evaluation that shows it'd be worse for Litracy to have me on board in this emotional state, than to let me go.'

'I see. You know, this never would have happened if you'd come to me in the first place. We let Aisha go because of this.'

'You let Aisha take an extended leave of absence because of health reasons.'

'There's a lot of work.'

'I've prepared a handover. Till I'm in the country, I can do it from home.'

'I'll have to discuss this with HR.'

'I already did. They agree I should not be around situations that antagonise me. The #metoo shook us all, and anymore stress, HR agrees, can be detrimental to my performance at JLF.' I hated using that as a shield, but I saw no way out in front of Farah and sure enough, that was the first and only time I saw my mother stumble. Just for a second.

'Oh. All right.'

'HR asked me what working with you was like. I told them it was fantastic and that I'd love a recommendation.'

'I'll think about that.'

'Thanks. I'll be leaving then. Bye.'

'This isn't over, Ruhi, we still live in the same house.'

'More than enough for me.'

I could feel her eyes on the back of my head as I picked up the last of my files and left her in an empty room, with no one to boss over.

~

Friday, 8 December

To Do:
• *Chill*

'Six tequila shots,' Rahul told the bartender. He'd insisted on taking me out Summerhouse Cafe to celebrate my freedom.

We had two each.

'Hang on, I'm getting a call.' It was Tejas wanting to FaceTime. I didn't want to speak with him, but I did want to see his face when I told him I quit.

'You'll never guess what.'

'Ruhi, you have to help me. I'm staying with Aisha.'

'You're staying with Aisha? Are you guys back together again?'

'Here, Ruhi.' Rahul slid up, putting the glass in my hand.

'Are you … are you in a bar, with that hipster?'

'Who're you calling a hipster?' Rahul butted in.

'Tejas, tell me what's up?'

'What are you doing drinking in the middle of the day?'

'It's 6.30 p.m. Anyway, Tejas! I quit. I quit that fucked-up job.'

'Yeah right.'

'She did, she really did,' said Rahul.

'You should thank me, I got all of us out of that thankless place,' I told Tejas.

'I guess. Look, something's wrong with Aisha.'

'What do you mean wrong?'

'She's stuck in her room all day, watching TV shows about skinny models. She doesn't bathe, has been drinking and smoking from the afternoon on.'

'Tejas, that's what some girls do when they're off work. Probably what I'm gonna be doing for the next month. Just because she isn't hopping to the salon on one leg isn't anything serious.'

'Ruhi, she's half her size. She's become a stick. She wants to go back.'

'Go back where?' I asked Tejas.

'She wants things to go back to the beginning. The way things were. You have to remind her. Remind her what it was like to feel happy rather than looking good,' he said. 'Can't you come over?'

'She won't make it, Tejas. We'll be partying till the weekend.' Rahul said.

'I'll call her later. We can't help her, Tejas. Help her help herself. I have to go.' I said, ending the call. 'Hey you, are you jealous? Of him?'

'Who me?' Rahul said. 'You were dating him. What about me?'

'What about you?' I was having an immense amount of fun, teasing him.

'How about dating me?'

Before I knew it, his lips were on my foolishly grinning smile and I was kissing him back in the middle of the bar. It wasn't as good as with Tejas and in a second I knew.

When we split for the night, I told him I wasn't ready what with all the Tejas drama. I had to deal with my own life. But I really wanted to see him that weekend. I thought he'd get pissed off and pouty but he was surprisingly okay. And so was I. That's when I realised, the 'loss' of my innocence wasn't going to happen the time I actually lost 'it'. It happened with my first heartbreak and had left me with something magnificent in return – the power to reject, or rather, the power to choose.

25

Dazed & Confused

– TEJAS –

Tuesday, 27 December

Life isn't easy for Aisha. Every day begins with waking up and looking in the mirror and feeling inadequate. Because every time she watches a movie or a TV show or an ad, she feels like an alien. I am writing this for her. For girls everywhere who are called fat. Whose 'fatness' stops them from being considered attractive. Who do not want to go on holidays and risk wearing swimsuits and bear the brunt of their non-attractiveness. Who are tired of getting passed over for their skinny friends. Life is a journey of a lifetime. We have to live it, not live in fear of other people who everyone else thinks are beautiful.

I've been here exactly a month now and for the first time Aisha had made an effort to look nice. Her hair smelled good. She'd taken a shirt of mine she used to like and tied a loop at the bottom, probably in an attempt to hide how much weight she'd lost. How she continues to do so with the amount of food I was cooking was a miracle.

We were having fish with a side of pasta. I usually ate one meal while writing and the other with her while watching a movie.

I knew something was up with the way she kept asking me how my writing was going and not interrupting but listening with her eyes glazing over. She used to do this before, when she was pretending to pay attention.

Promptly she said, 'Tejas, I've been thinking.'

'That's good, for a change.'

'I'm grateful you've been here.'

'You were, for me.'

'The plaster will come off tomorrow but I will need physiotherapy and stuff. Why don't you stay on till the middle of January?'

'I guess I could.'

'And another thing, I've decided we could date again.'

It would have been the easiest thing to say yes. But I wasn't going to do that anymore. She and Ruhi were not toys I could play with at will. I dealt with my shit on my own. So did Ruhi. Aisha had to cross the finish line on her own.

'No, Aisha, I'm here as a friend.'

'Aren't you trying to get me back?' Her face fell.

'Look, I care about you. A lot. You have to get out of this hole you've dug yourself into,' I said.

'What hole? I'm absolutely amazing. I'm back to my old self – who I used to be,' Aisha said.

'Just because your weight is the same, doesn't mean you're the same person!'

'What else does it mean, Tejas?'

'I've never met anyone like you, who's affected me so much. But this is the time for you to focus on yourself. I'm not saying work if you don't wanna work. All I'm saying is at least live a life you enjoy. Read, write about fashion if you like it so much. Watch things, movies, documentaries, not just silly mind-numbing shows all the time. I don't care if you waste all the time you have, but do it gloriously.'

'You are still as manipulative as you were the day I left Litracy. I, I don't know what you want. I know what I want and I asked you. If you don't want to date me, be honest. Don't make it conditional.'

I knew I'd lost her at this point.

'Okay, you know what, it's me. I've just been getting my writing on track. Okay? I will consider dating you again once I'm sure my writing is on a roll and I'm not gonna hurt you again.'

She scoffed. Then her face softened when she realised I wasn't being sarcastic.

'I can help you through it, like I did before.'

I wanted to laugh. 'I'm not ready. I'll just do the exact same thing and spoil it again.'

'Why don't you sit out in the sun and watch that cat you've been feeding, or sunbathe? He's getting fatter every week. I'll air out your room till then.'

'Fine.'

There was a funky smell in her room. Things were as usual. Unwashed glasses, plates and ashtrays in corners and under the bed. The shelves were dusty and the bedsheets smelled like they weren't fresh at all. The room was dark and cold despite the radiator. I pulled the curtains open and let the sunlight stream in. Small wine bottles lined the floor next to magazines. And I thought I was a lone drinker.

I attacked the room with a duster and cleaning spray. Thank goodness Aisha had a vacuum cleaner.

I wiped the dust off the magazines and got started on her bedside table. I pulled open the drawer – there was a lighter and two packets of cigarettes. I pocketed them both. I saw a notebook, a pink faux leather dairy. I could take a peek. Maybe if I read it, I'd know a bit more of what was going on in Aisha's head.

After a few minutes of reading, I'd read enough.

'Aisha, what the hell is this?' I stormed out with her diary in my hand.

'You read my diary? You've never read my diary. Even when we were dating.'

'I'm staying here to help you and you pull this crap. Throwing up after eating? You're smarter than this Aisha, you used to be the smartest person I knew. You never took shit from me or Ruhi. Don't take it from yourself.'

'You stopped dating me when I was fat.'

'I stopped dating you 'coz you stopped taking care of yourself. I can't even stand to be around you right now.'

'Fine. Leave.'

'I will.'

I had a good mind to pack my stuff and go home but I took a walk instead. Her cast would be off soon so I decided to stick on for a few more days. No matter what shit she's doing to herself, she shouldn't have to be alone on New Year's Day.

26

Irony of a Looking Glass

– AISHA –

Friday, 31 December

Tejas was quiet all the way to the hospital and back. He didn't even sit in the same room with me when they drilled my cast open. He hadn't said a word besides texting me he'd be out of here on 1st January. He'd stopped eating with me too and gave me a tray in my room as if I were a resident in a mental institution.

It was New Year's Eve and he had plans so he ordered me food and left.

I guess he and I thought that after my cast was gone, I'd feel better. It was weird but I felt helpless – more so, even.

I had no excuse to sit in bed all day long but I did.

What really annoyed me was that I wasn't getting used to this thin person in the mirror. There was no difference in my head between now and when I was a fat person.

I sat with my laptop and took out a glass of wine Tejas had kept aside and hidden the rest. A single glass. At least he didn't discover the wine bottle in my shoebox.

I took my time and washed my hair, put on makeup, found my favourite dress and heels. Everything finally fit. I think I'd done it. On New Year's Eve, I was going to toast my best self. I had turned things around.

Tejas had left what I thought was the worst movie for me in the world today – *Shallow Hal*. I couldn't stop watching it for some weird reason. It was like staring at someone ugly, you couldn't move your gaze away.

The movie was one of the most depressing things I'd ever seen. I had to cheer myself up so I finished half the bottle of wine while watching *Next Top Model* till 11 p.m.

At midnight I went into my dressing room. I began taking selfies in my dress to jumpstart a new blog when I tripped and fell on my knees. I'd tripped over an old box of diaries. My plan was to bid my fat self goodbye forever that night and wake up a fresh new person. What better way than to remember and let go of the old me.

ᇰ

Saturday, 1 January

When I woke up, it was 6 a.m. I was in my dressing room. Tejas wasn't back yet.

How drunk was I last night? My left foot was sore from having slept with the heels on in an awkward position.

I took a good look at myself in the mirror. I was thin. My clothes fit but I did not look pretty from any angle. I was also ugly. Had I not realised this and not seen the mirror properly for a month? My hair was dull and limp. I couldn't balance in those heels anymore, what was I doing wearing them while recovering from a fracture? I looked old and my dark circles were horrendous. I had breakouts, my skin was patchy. I looked like a zombie.

It wasn't the same. I had been kidding myself.

I struggled to understand. I'd done everything, stopped eating, thrown up after every meal. What else did I have to do to look good?

My diaries were spread around me.

An entry dated May, the day I first joined Litracy, said, 'As long as I look this way, the world will be at my feet. It got me here and it's going to take me higher.'

I read more. Every single thing I read was about how I looked. Not one entry was about my accomplishments. Was my confidence a sham? Was I a mannequin, not a person? Every single thing in my room was related to my appearance. There was no photo of my friends, no degrees, posters, achievements. Just pictures of myself.

I wandered around the room. I was not these magazines, I was not these clothes, I was not that bottle of wine, or those shoes. I could be all of these but I was more.

I didn't recognise the person in the mirror in the dressing room. I punched it. It broke on my hand.

I recoiled from the shock of having shattered it and knelt down. I noticed blood on the magazine and diary I was holding. I didn't realise I was cut, I was still a little hungover and shaky. I noticed a piece of the mirror on the floor. I picked it up and held it next to my wrist.

Blood from my hand smeared it. My face reflected blood in that tiny cracked piece of glass. I could end it all right now.

My parents would be happier without me. Anyway, their problems had always been bigger than mine. I could write a letter to Tejas saying this wasn't his fault. Ruhi had her own life.

It was an option.

The other option was to move on and probably become a fat and ugly person and be okay with it. I could not picture myself like that. I couldn't stand my room any longer.

I couldn't bear to face it. I began taking my things and dumping them outside my room. The cat was watching me from a corner. I gave him quite a show. I made a mountain of my magazines and gave it a good kick. I added all my tight clothes and skimpy outfits. I took off the dress I was wearing. I added the multitude of mirrors and mock model photos of myself to the lot.

My room looked empty and my wardrobe too. Like a void, exactly how I felt.

I thought I would be free but I felt empty and breathless.

I got out of the corridor and into the garden. The fresh morning breeze helped me with my hangover. I was drenched in sweat. The world was asleep or probably passed out. I walked in my garden barefoot, till I felt lighter and lighter like I was rising up.

Every time I thought of my empty room, I would freak out. So I stopped and sat in the garden and looked at the leaves and the flowers and the cat.

My mind kept telling me I had to choose the feeling which came with looking bad. Something felt wrong with that.

I examined myself again. There was nothing wrong with wanting to look good. I was not a hollow person despite everything.

It was also okay to not like the person in the mirror. Nobody was perfect. We all had our flaws. Even diamonds. I didn't have to like them.

I could not stand my chubby self and that was okay. I could love it anyway.

If we accepted our shortcomings, nobody would ever hit the gym. I could acknowledge that I was addicted to food and now I was addicted to a mirror image. But neither of those were of the standards I would accept.

The blood on my hand had dried. I was hungry. I decided to start my day off by cooking a meal for myself.

I went in and started to make tea. I boiled the water. It felt good to stand and wait for it though my leg was hurting and my head felt really dizzy because I was so hungover.

Who would I be, what would I do? That thought made my head spin in a good way. I dropped the teacup and slipped on the spilled water. I wasn't sure if I was fainting again.

'Well, that's a sight I didn't expect,' Tejas said, entering and helping me up. He saw the broken cup and talked while he cleaned up.

'I bet Ruhi you'd be fine by January. She told me you'd be fine before the New Year.'

'Well, you won. Thanks for betting against me.'

'Let's get you something to eat, other than chocolate,' Tejas said.

'Chocolate?'

Then I noticed the counter.

There was a framed photo of myself from Bhutan, happy with Ruhi and Tejas on either side. There were chocolates all around the photo and a card from both of them saying they were looking forward to me being my 'happy self, not this ghost of a girl'.

It all made sense, it just fit.

'Tejas, I don't know where to start,' I said. 'You've stayed here, you've cleaned, cooked, I just...'

'For now, just chill.'

'I don't know what to do, there is so much going on.'

'I know, I know. It's okay. You got through it. I'll help you figure out the rest. Are you ready to let go?' he asked me, and I followed him outside.

He gave me his lighter and said to start when I was ready. So I took the first magazine from fifteen years ago and lit it and threw it into the barbecue. I threw all the magazines in one by one. Then my clothes. Then my diaries. I got my weighing scale too but Tejas put that in his car, saying he'd get rid of it for me.

'Now what?' he said.

'Breakfast,' I replied.

27

A Real Sweet Life

– RUHI –

Sunday, 18 February

To Do:
- *Zero in on online model to adopt from final selection*
- *Brainstorming sesh & team drinks on Wednesday*
- *Explore possibility of app in this year*
- *Consider going for low-residency publishing Master's end of year*

'I finally did it.'

'On vacation?' Aisha asked me. Tejas was looking at his hands then his shoes, unsure of where to settle his gaze, at Aisha or me. We were sitting in the cafe in Khan Market, Tejas's favourite.

'If not in Bhutan, then Singapore it is,' I said, nudging Tejas. 'It's okay, we can laugh about it now.'

The three of us were meeting after two months. I had extended my holiday in Singapore and spent some time there. I'd never travelled on my own before and I had a lot of time to think and figure out things.

Aisha had written a long email to me at the beginning of the year, telling me how she'd come out of the bad place she was in. She looked serene, a word I never thought I'd use for her. Her face was filling out and she'd started learning yoga and had been managing her diet again. She still had gym nightmares though, she'd said, but according to Maya, they were just old fears, and would slowly fade.

Tejas was still staying with her and they were finally having fun. They insisted they weren't dating. I wondered how long that would last.

'What are your plans?' I asked him.

'All the scribbles I'd been making for months, it turned out I had to write what was happening around me. I'm not the kind of writer to pull things out of thin air, at least not yet. I'm already on my second draft,' Tejas said.

'No prizes for guessing whom the book is about,' Aisha said.

'It's loosely inspired by you guys.'

'Do you want me to look at it?' I volunteered.

'Only if you want to,' he said.

'And you, Aisha?'

'Well, I had a long talk with Maya in January, came clean about all of last year. I'm setting up a food and fitness blog with her. It will be a one-stop shop for eating and living well. So I just won't have the time.'

'And your own blog?'

'It's back online. My real fans have stuck around. I'm going to continue with it too, for fun. And you? What is Ruhi Singh going to do, after leaving Litracy in style?'

'I'm starting my own publishing house.'

'What, really?'

'Well, e-publishing and a combination of print-on-demand. WD is closing the Litracy imprint, but I've retained my author network and designers. A lot of them and upcoming authors are keen on being online.'

'Way to go, Ruhi. That's awesome,' Aisha said.

'I can consider your manuscript for it, Tejas.'

'Wow, really?'

'If I like it.'

'You know you will.'

It was going to be a real sweet life.

Acknowledgments

I thank Fay Weldon, my writing mentor for being the ray of sunshine during my gloomy winter writing days in England; Bambo Soyinka for being a wonderful source of encouragement always; Priya Kapoor and Neelam Narula for making my days at Roli Books a joy to write about; Kanishka, Neelini, and Lipika for championing me more than my book at times; Prerna and the entire HarperCollins team without whom this book wouldn't have been possible; my four wonderful grandparents and extended family for their regular encouragement; Avneet, Saloni, Devyani, Vijayraj, Suhani, Gaetano and Simi for their constant support during the writing of the book; my Bath Writer's group of Mary, Celia and Kay for reading the first draft; Madhavi and Kyoshi Rahul for helping me focus with yoga and karate respectively; all the well-wishers I came across while writing the book; and lastly Simba, my writing dog.

About the Author

Neharika Gupta is a martial arts practitioner, yogi, poet and writer. She worked in publishing for a year before shifting to writing full-time. She lives in Delhi with her parents and three dogs. She holds a B.A. (H) in English Literature from Lady Shri Ram College for Women and an M.A. in Creative Writing from Bath Spa University, UK. *Adulting* is her debut novel. She also writes at neharikagupta.com.